Crack

DRUGS The Straight Facts

Alcohol
Alzheimer's and Memory Drugs
Anti-Anxiety Drugs
Antidepressants
Barbiturates
Birth Control Pills
Botox® and Other Cosmetic Drugs
Cancer Drugs
Cocaine
Codeine
Crack
Date Rape Drugs
Ecstasy
Heroin
HIV/AIDS Treatment Drugs
LSD
Marijuana
Methamphetamine
Morphine
Nicotine
Opium
Peyote and Mescaline
Prescription Pain Relievers
Quaaludes
Sleep Aids
Weight Loss Drugs

■ DRUGS
The Straight Facts

Crack

M. Foster Olive, Ph.D.

Consulting Editor
David J. Triggle
University Professor
School of Pharmacy and Pharmaceutical Sciences
State University of New York at Buffalo

CHELSEA HOUSE
P U B L I S H E R S
An imprint of Infobase Publishing

Drugs The Straight Facts: Crack

Copyright © 2008 by Infobase Publishing

Chelsea House
An imprint of Infobase Publishing
132 West 31st Street
New York NY 10001

Library of Congress Cataloging-in-Publication Data
Olive, M. Foster.
  Crack / M. Foster Olive, David J. Triggle.
    p. cm. — (Drugs: the straight facts)
  Includes bibliographical references and index.
  ISBN-13: 978-0-7910-9710-6 (alk. paper)
  ISBN-10: 0-7910-9710-2 (alk. paper)
  1. Crack (Drug) I. Triggle, D. J. II. Title. III. Series.

  RC568.C6O532 2008
  616.86'47—dc22
                 2007052332

Chelsea House books are available at special discounts when purchased in bulk quantities for businesses, associations, institutions, or sales promotions. Please call our Special Sales Department in New York at (212) 967-8800 or (800) 322-8755.

You can find Chelsea House on the World Wide Web at
http://www.chelseahouse.com

Text and cover design by Terry Mallon and Keith Trego

Printed in the United States of America

Bang EJB 10 9 8 7 6 5 4 3 2 1

This book is printed on acid-free paper.

All links and Web addresses were checked and verified to be correct at the time of publication. Because of the dynamic nature of the Web, some addresses and links may have changed since publication and may no longer be valid.

Table of Contents

The Use and Abuse of Drugs

The issues associated with drug use and abuse in contemporary society are vexing subjects, fraught with political agendas and ideals that often obscure essential information that teens need to know to have intelligent discussions about how to best deal with the problems associated with drug use and abuse. *Drugs: The Straight Facts* aims to provide this essential information through straightforward explanations of how an individual drug or group of drugs works in both therapeutic and nontherapeutic conditions, with historical information about the use and abuse of specific drugs, with discussion of drug policies in the United States, and with an ample list of further reading.

From the start, the series uses the word "drug" to describe psychoactive substances that are used for medicinal or non-medicinal purposes. Included in this broad category are substances that are legal or illegal. It is worth noting that humans have used many of these substances for hundreds, if not thousands, of years. For example, traces of marijuana and cocaine have been found in Egyptian mummies; the use of peyote and Amanita fungi has long been a component of religious ceremonies worldwide; and alcohol production and consumption have been an integral part of many human cultures' social and religious ceremonies. One can speculate about why early human societies chose to use such drugs. Perhaps, anything that could provide relief from the harshness of life—anything that could make the poor conditions and fatigue associated with hard work easier to bear—was considered a welcome tonic. Life was likely to be, according to seventeenth century English philosopher Thomas Hobbes, "poor, nasty, brutish, and short." One can also speculate about modern human societies' continued use and abuse of drugs. Whatever the reasons, the consequences of sustained drug use are not insignificant—addiction, overdose, incarceration, and drug wars—and must be dealt with by an informed citizenry.

The problem that faces our society today is how to break the connection between our demand for drugs and the willingness of largely outside countries to supply this highly profitable trade. This is the same problem we have faced since narcotics and cocaine were outlawed by the Harrison Narcotic Act of 1914, and we have yet to defeat it despite current expenditures of approximately $20 billion per year on "the war on drugs." The first step in meeting any challenge is always an intelligent and informed citizenry. The purpose of this series is to educate our readers so that they can make informed decisions about issues related to drugs and drug abuse.

SUGGESTED ADDITIONAL READING

Courtwright, David T. *Forces of Habit, Drugs and the Making of the Modern World.* Cambridge, Mass.: Harvard University Press, 2001. David T. Courtwright is professor of history at the University of North Florida.

Davenport-Hines, Richard. *The Pursuit of Oblivion: A Global History of Narcotics.* New York: Norton, 2002. The author is a professional historian and a member of the Royal Historical Society.

Huxley, Aldous. *Brave New World.* New York: Harper & Row, 1932. Huxley's book, written in 1932, paints a picture of a cloned society devoted only to the pursuit of happiness.

David J. Triggle, Ph.D.
University Professor
School of Pharmacy and Pharmaceutical Sciences
State University of New York at Buffalo

1

An Overview of Crack Cocaine

I smoke and I smoke and I smoke. I get so high, I'm in a faraway, different world. It's a better world. A heavenly domain . . . everything is wonderful. Only when the stone runs out I am miserable . . . very miserable. I need more stone to keep this high going and avoid a crash. By 5:00 A.M. I'm out of stone again. . . . I've spent $200 in the past 18 hours. . . . The high is gone, and I'm feeling sweaty, shaky and disoriented . . . lonely, depressed, full of anxiety and scared. I begin to cry as I drive along (to work), slowly and surely having to admit to myself that I am now a slave to this stuff and my Master will be calling on me and demanding my submissive service all the live-long day.

—Marvin Wilson[1]

When one hears the term *crackhead* (in reference to someone who uses **crack** cocaine), images of a strung-out, homeless junkie who had an abusive upbringing might come to mind. People who use crack are not always poor, however, nor do they always come from dysfunctional families or abusive childhoods. Crack knows no socioeconomic boundaries. In his autobiographical book, *I Romanced the Stone*, Marvin Wilson details how he was once a successful businessman with a wife, three children, a nice home, and a six-figure income. His life, however, started to unravel when his business took a nosedive, and the stress of losing his comfortable lifestyle caused him to drift apart from his wife and sink into depression. In an attempt to lift himself out of the psychological hole he had fallen into, he befriended a prostitute

Figure 1.1   The coca plant. *(© Jorge Uzon/Corbis.)*

who also happened to be a crack-cocaine user. Eventually, Marvin tried smoking crack, and within a few tries he was hooked and eventually developed a crack habit that cost him between $100 and $200 a day.

FORMS OF COCAINE

The use of cocaine dates back several thousand years, when inhabitants of South America used to chew on leaves of the **coca plant** (*Erythroxylan coca*) for its pleasurable effects and its ability to allow them to work harder, with more energy, and less hunger and fatigue.[2] Even today some South Americans still use cocaine in many cultural and religious aspects of their lives, often referring to the coca plant as a "gift from the gods."

The coca plant is indigenous to South American countries such as Colombia, Bolivia, and Peru. Although all cocaine is derived from the coca plant, the drug is used in many different forms. Some people, such as those living in certain regions of South America, chew the raw leaves of the coca plant by placing the leaves between the cheek and gum, much like chewing tobacco. Alternatively, the leaves of the coca plant can be ground into a **paste** that is then dried and smoked in cigarettes. The bulky nature of coca leaves and paste, however, makes it difficult to traffic and smuggle to other parts of the world, and thus use of these types of cocaine are rarely found outside of South America.

When coca paste is mixed with a strong acid called hydrochloric acid, it can be concentrated into a purer and more potent form known as **cocaine hydrochloride**. Since this form of cocaine is more concentrated than that from coca paste or leaves, it is less bulky and thus more easily smuggled in and out of various countries. Cocaine hydrochloride is the primary ingredient found in powdered cocaine, which is white in color and has the consistency of powdered sugar or baking soda. Cocaine hydrochloride is usually snorted through a short tube or straw into the nostrils.

In the 1980s cocaine manufacturers and chemists found a new way to make cocaine even more potent and concentrated than the hydrochloride form. Through a procedure called **freebasing**, chemists could get rid of the "hydrochloride" part of the cocaine, resulting in cocaine that is almost 100 percent pure. This procedure, however, involves lengthy chemical processing and the use of dangerous chemicals such as ether, which if not fully evaporated prior to smoking the **freebase** cocaine, could cause an explosion. In 1980, comedian Richard Pryor was seriously burned when flames erupted while he was trying to smoke freebase cocaine.

Not too long after the appearance of freebase cocaine came an alternative called crack cocaine. Crack is a crystallized form of cocaine that is made by adding baking soda and water to cocaine hydrochloride and allowing it to dry. A common misconception is that crack cocaine is the same as freebase cocaine, when in fact they are different chemical forms of the same drug. Crack cocaine looks like small, off-white stones or

Figure 1.2   Cocaine, in the form of a fine white powder, is most commonly taken by snorting it. *(U.S. Drug Enforcement Administration.)*

pebbles, hence its common nickname "rock," and is often sold in small plastic bags or glass vials.

Crack cocaine is most often smoked in homemade **crack pipes**, which come in all shapes and sizes. The crack pipe usually consists of a long tube made of steel or glass, which is sometimes connected to a laboratory flask or beaker from a chemistry lab or store. Attached to the tube or beaker is a type of funnel or cup for holding the crack cocaine. When crack is heated with a cigarette lighter or small blowtorch, it gives off fumes that the user inhales through the tube. Smoking is the most common way crack cocaine is taken. Some cocaine users, however, may choose to crush the crack into a powder, continuously heat it in a spoon placed over an open flame until it melts into a liquid (often with the help of adding a little bit of lemon juice[3]). The liquid can then be drawn into a syringe and injected intravenously, a procedure often called "slamming," "mainlining," or "shooting up."

EFFECTS OF COCAINE AND CRACK ON THE MIND AND BODY

Although the effects of cocaine can vary slightly as a function of the chemical form and the method by which it is taken, the general effects of the drug are fairly consistent, and include:

- increased heart rate and blood pressure

- dilation of the pupils

- constriction of the airways

- euphoria and "high" (feelings of pleasure and well-being, often described as a "whole body orgasm")

- increased alertness, energy, and movement (pacing, fidgeting)

- increased desire to socialize

- increased self-esteem

- increased physical sensations

- increased sexual desire

- increased impulsivity

- increased body temperature and sweating

- decreased appetite

While most people experience a pleasurable high after taking cocaine, repeated taking of the drug can lead to some not-so-pleasurable feelings. Some chronic cocaine users may feel nervous, paranoid, or even experience **hallucinations**. Others many feel as though they have bugs crawling under their skin (so-called coke bugs).

Figure 1.3 Crack cocaine is a crystallized form of cocaine that is most commonly taken by smoking it through a pipe. *(U.S. Drug Enforcement Administration.)*

The type of experience one has after taking cocaine can vary widely as a function of one's personality, genetic makeup, past experience with cocaine, and the environment and people with which the drug is taken. For example, people who tend to have aggressive personalities might be prone to become even more aggressive and engage in fighting after taking cocaine than people who have more easygoing personalities. Certain genetic factors may also influence the type of experience one has after smoking crack; for example, some people may be genetically more sensitive to the effects of cocaine than others (just as some people have different levels of sensitivity to alcohol), and thus may experience a more intense high. Generally, people who experience an extremely intense euphoria after smoking crack are the most likely to pursue further crack use, whereas a person who has a bad experience and becomes paranoid may continue to have such bad experiences with crack that eventually they perhaps turn to a different drug. Finally, people who smoke crack in a group "party" setting tend to become more sociable and talkative, whereas people who like to smoke crack by themselves may feel introverted and unsociable after smoking crack.

The route by which cocaine or crack is taken also determines how quickly the high is obtained. When cocaine is chewed, enzymes present in saliva are needed to break down the cells of the coca leaf and release the cocaine molecules into the mouth, which is then slowly absorbed into the bloodstream through the gums or the lining of the cheek. Similarly, when cocaine powder is snorted, the cocaine is slowly absorbed through the linings of the nasal cavity. As a result, the peak onset of the high following chewing or snorting cocaine is not achieved for approximately one to two hours and is only experienced as a mild or moderate high. This high lasts for several hours, however, because not all of the cocaine enters the bloodstream at once. In contrast, when cocaine is taken intravenously or smoked (like crack), the onset of the high is much quicker (often within a few seconds) because the cocaine more rapidly enters the bloodstream (directly in the case of intravenous injection, or by passing into capillaries of the lungs in the case of smoked crack), and the euphoria is extremely intense because of the rapid rate at which the cocaine reaches the brain (more on this topic in Chapter 2). The duration of the high after smoking crack or injecting dissolved cocaine, however, is fairly short—usually lasting only an hour or two—because all of the cocaine gets into the bloodstream at once and is cleared from the blood by the liver. When the cocaine high wears off, it makes the user "crash"—feeling irritable, depressed, fatigued, anxious, and craving more cocaine. Experienced crack addicts often anticipate the onset of the symptoms of the crash, which leads to more cocaine use and perpetuates the cycle of addiction.

CRACK SLANG TERMINOLOGY

As with any illegal drug, crack has many street names. It is most commonly referred to as "rock" because of its rock-like appearance. Other general names for crack include *hard white, white, caps, caviar, crills, barneys, yeyo, poprocks, foo-foo dust, jacks,* or *boulya.* Crack that is sold in larger rocks can be referred to as *bricks, boulders,* or *eight-ball.* Crack rocks that are very small or only resemble shavings of rocks are referred to as *crumbs, shake,* or *kibbles and bits.*

Sometimes crack is sealed into plastic bags and stamped with a "brand name" that users can ask for specifically. This brand name also gives the user a false sense of security that the crack is actually of higher quality. Some brand names of crack that were common in the early 1990s in New York City were "Bogey" (named after Humphrey Bogart in the movie *Key Largo*), "Noriega's Holiday" (named after the former Panamanian dictator Manuel Noriega who was deposed for his involvement in cocaine trafficking), or "Pablo" (named after Pablo Escobar, the former head of a large Colombian drug cartel).

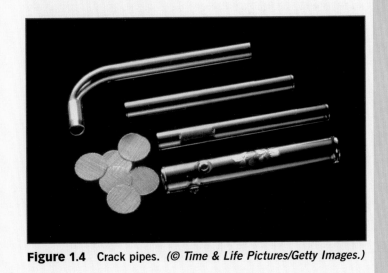

Figure 1.4   Crack pipes. *(© Time & Life Pictures/Getty Images.)*

THE CRACK SUBCULTURE

Since its introduction into society in the mid-1980s, crack cocaine has created a distinct subculture among the people who use it. Crack cocaine is relatively inexpensive (enough crack for three or four uses costs as little as $10–$20), which makes it more attractive for people without a large amount of spare cash, particularly young people and the economically disadvantaged. In contrast, powdered cocaine is much more expensive, costing the heavy user several hundred dollars a day. The relatively low price for an intense crack high is one of the primary reasons crack gained popularity so quickly and remained widely used, particularly within poverty-stricken areas of large metropolitan cities such as New York, Los Angeles, Miami, Atlanta, Chicago, and Houston, which are considered the **primary market areas** for cocaine distribution.[4] Cities such as Baltimore; Boston; Detroit; Newark, N.J.; Philadelphia; Phoenix; and Tucson, Ariz., are also areas where use of crack cocaine is prevalent, but are not considered cocaine primary market areas.

The instant popularity of crack cocaine gave rise to what is known as the **crack house**, a place where people go to buy crack cocaine as well as find a safe place to smoke it. Crack houses are similar to opium dens, where during the nineteenth century (at the peak of opium's popularity) people used to go to buy and smoke the drug. Crack houses are also similar to "shooting galleries" or "dope houses," where people go to buy and use heroin. Crack houses are primarily found in poor, inner-city neighborhoods where the frequency of crack use is greater than in more wealthy suburban areas. Crack houses are usually old, dilapidated apartments, homes, shacks, or abandoned buildings. There are even nicknames for different types of crack houses. For example, places where large amounts of crack are manufactured and sold are called "castles," since they are fortified with steel doors, locks, barred windows, and workers armed with guns. A "resort" or "brothel" is a crack house where sex is often traded in exchange for crack. Prostitutes who engage in sexual acts in exchange for crack are often referred to as "crack whores" or "skeezers." In addition, there may be somewhat of an organizational hierarchy within the crack house, with a "house man" who is in charge of a particular crack house, along with a "runner" who helps the house man run errands or manufacture and distribute the crack rocks.[5]

2

Why Is Crack So Addictive?

Dwayne, a 25-year-old former crack addict now in a residential reha-bilitation program, was having lunch with some of his fellow residents and talking about his past life on the street as a crack addict. "For me, it wasn't just that I was taking drugs. I had taken lots of drugs before: speed, Ecstasy, LSD—you name it. But this crack stuff, it consumed me. It became a way of life. As a teenager, I used to think about all the things I wanted to be when I finished college. I wanted to coach high school hoops and teach math. But after I got into crack, none of that mattered any more. The only thing that was important to me was scoring my next hit. And I would do anything to get it, even if it meant hurting someone."

"Dang, bro . . . you had it bad," says Shawn, a recovering alco-holic who had befriended Dwayne in the six weeks they had been in rehab together. "Thank God I only stuck to the bottle. I was pretty messed up too, but at least I could function and still go to work at the construction site."

"Yeah, I know. That rock, it was my worst demon. If I had a chance to go back and do anything in my life over again, I would have stayed away from rock that first time my buddy offered it to me. I was hooked within two or three days."

Of all the intoxicating drugs that are available—cocaine, heroin, methamphetamine, alcohol—crack seems to be one of the most addictive. People often report that they become addicted after the second or third time trying crack. Why is this form of cocaine so tremendously addictive?

CRACK REACHES THE BRAIN ALMOST IMMEDIATELY

Laboratory animals, such as rats or mice, are often used in studying the effects of cocaine on the brain and how it changes behavior. Typically, the rat or mouse is implanted with an intravenous **catheter** and is placed into an experimental apparatus where it is trained to press a lever in order to receive an infusion of a liquid solution containing cocaine. Researchers can study various phenomena, such as how many times the rodent will self-administer the drug in a given amount of time, or how hard it will work to obtain a cocaine infusion. Such studies have shown that rodents tend to prefer the cocaine when it is infused at a faster rate than when it is infused at a slower rate.[6] This has led scientists to hypothesize that the faster the drug enters the bloodstream, the greater its pleasurable effects.

Similar studies have been performed in human cocaine addicts. Many treatment clinics, hospitals, and university research programs recruit cocaine addicts to volunteer to participate in research studies on how cocaine affects the body and the brain, and on the development of therapies to treat cocaine addiction. Such studies, when conducted under carefully controlled and monitored conditions, have shown that cocaine produces the quickest and most intense high when it is smoked—as crack cocaine is—followed closely by when it is injected intravenously.

COCAINE ACTIVATES THE BRAIN'S PLEASURE CENTERS

The brain contains various regions that are considered to be "pleasure" or "reward" centers. These centers are naturally activated by things that are necessary for our survival, such as food and sex. These regions of the brain are also activated by all drugs that are addictive, including cocaine, amphetamines, heroin, nicotine, and alcohol. Today, most scientists agree that addictive drugs hijack the brain's own natural reward circuitry, taking control over it and making the drug user unable to

CHOOSING CRACK OVER INTRAVENOUS COCAINE: A LABORATORY STUDY

Cocaine is taken in many forms, usually snorting cocaine powder, intravenously injecting a cocaine solution, or smoking crack. In an effort to examine which route is the most "likeable" and produces the most pleasurable effects, Richard Foltin and Marian Fischman conducted an intriguing laboratory study at Johns Hopkins University (Foltin and Fischman, 1992).[7] Male cocaine addicts were brought into a drug-abuse research clinic and were allowed to sample various doses of either smoked or intravenous cocaine. After this sampling test, the addicts were allowed to choose up to five doses of either crack or intravenous cocaine, and then asked to rate their subjective feelings of high after taking the drug. The researchers found that the cocaine addicts reliably chose smoked cocaine over intravenous cocaine, and it produced the greatest high. Thus, even in a controlled laboratory setting, crack is preferred over intravenous cocaine, and produces more intense and pleasurable effects.

So why would smoking cocaine produce greater effects than intravenous administration? Wouldn't intravenous cocaine enter the bloodstream the quickest? The answer has to do with the anatomy of the circulatory system. When crack smoke is inhaled, it passes easily from the small air sacs in the lungs (called alveoli) into the tiny capillaries in the lungs, which flow to the heart via the pulmonary vein. After the blood in the pulmonary vein enters the heart, it is pumped directly into the aorta, a major branch of which (the carotid artery) supplies blood directly to the brain. If cocaine were injected intravenously, however—say in a vein in the forearm, leg, or foot—it might have to travel through the entire circulatory system prior to returning to the heart and reaching the brain via the aorta and carotid artery. For this reason, smoked crack cocaine reaches the brain quicker than intravenously injected cocaine.

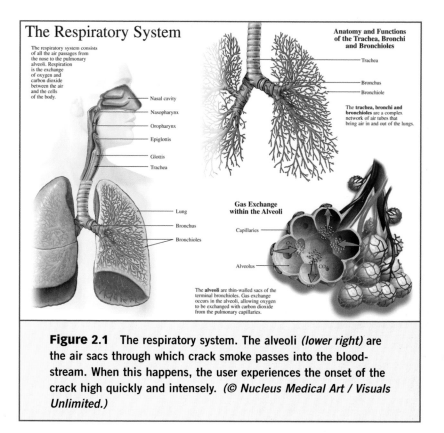

The Respiratory System

The respiratory system consists of all the air passages from the nose to the pulmonary alveoli. Respiration is the exchange of oxygen and carbon dioxide between the air and the cells of the body.

- Nasal cavity
- Nasopharynx
- Oropharynx
- Epiglottis
- Glottis
- Trachea
- Lung
- Bronchus
- Bronchioles

Anatomy and Functions of the Trachea, Bronchi and Bronchioles

- Trachea
- Bronchus
- Bronchiole

The **trachea, bronchi and bronchioles** are a complex network of air tubes that bring air in and out of the lungs.

Gas Exchange within the Alveoli

- Capillaries
- Alveolus

The **alveoli** are thin-walled sacs of the terminal bronchioles. Gas exchange occurs in the alveoli, allowing oxygen to be exchanged with carbon dioxide from the pulmonary capillaries.

Figure 2.1   The respiratory system. The alveoli *(lower right)* are the air sacs through which crack smoke passes into the bloodstream. When this happens, the user experiences the onset of the crack high quickly and intensely. *(© Nucleus Medical Art / Visuals Unlimited.)*

control his or her desire and intake of drugs or alcohol. The end result is addiction.

In the brain, nerve cells (**neurons**) carry electrical signals along wire-like nerve fibers called **axons**. At the end of each axon is a mushroom-shaped nerve ending called a **synaptic terminal**. Axons in the brain can range from less than a millimeter in length to up to several centimeters. When the electrical signal traveling down the axon reaches the synaptic terminal, it causes chemical messengers (called **neurotransmitters**) to be released and secreted onto nearby receiving neurons. This junction between a synaptic terminal and a nearby receiving neuron is called a **synapse**; there are literally billions of synapses in the brain, and each neuron can have as many as 10,000 different synapses on it. After neurotransmitters are released, they diffuse away from the synaptic terminal into the synapse and encounter proteins (called **receptors**) on the surface of nearby receiving neurons. Receptors are specific proteins that are designed to recognize specific neurotransmitters. When activated by neurotransmitters, these receptors can cause the receiving nerve cell on which they reside to either become activated (so that it passes along the electrical signal) or inhibited (so that it doesn't pass the signal along). In order for the nerve to terminate the chemical signal, it reabsorbs the neurotransmitter back into the synaptic terminal so it can be reused for future nerve impulses.

One of the central "pleasure" centers in the brain is called the **ventral tegmental area** (VTA), which is located deep within the brain. The VTA is densely populated by neurons that produce the neurotransmitter **dopamine**. Neurons in the VTA send long axons to various regions in the forward part of the brain, particularly regions such as the **nucleus accumbens** and **frontal cortex**. When the brain receives input that activates neurons in the VTA, this causes the release of dopamine, the result of which is the sensation of pleasure or satisfaction. This pleasure circuitry is activated by natural things we find satisfying, such as food, sex, and interpersonal interactions. Such things are necessary for our survival as a species, and nature has made sure we engage in such behaviors by making them pleasurable experiences. Drugs such as crack, however, also activate these pleasure centers within the brain and eventually cause this brain circuitry to function improperly, leading the drug user to seek out and take drugs at the expense of engaging in normal behaviors that this pleasure circuit was intended to use. In other words, addictive drugs such as crack and heroin hijack the normal pleasure circuits within the brain and change them in such a way that the person ends up hooked on drugs rather than behaviors that are intended to help us survive.

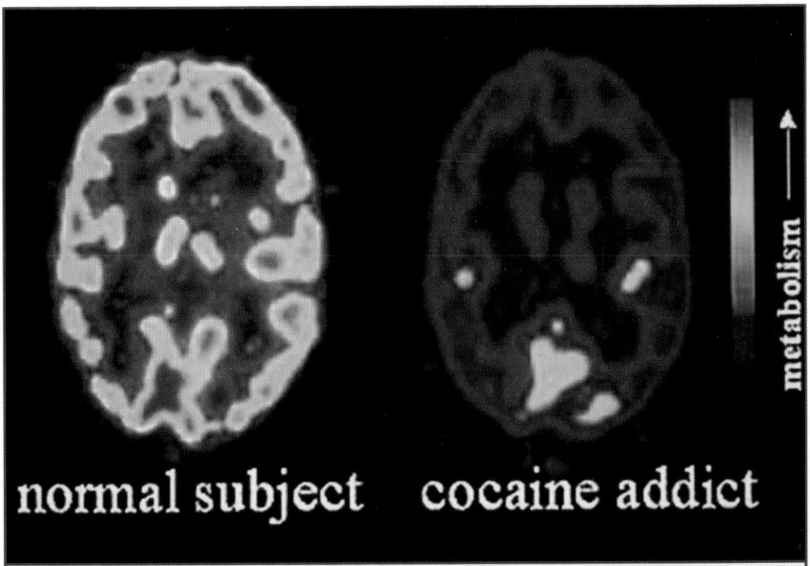

normal subject   cocaine addict

Figure 2.2 These positron emission tomography scans (PET scans) show the difference in brain activity between a person who is addicted to crack and a person who does not use the drug. (© *Science VU / Visuals Unlimited.*)

So how does crack cocaine activate the brain's pleasure centers? Once dopamine is released by synaptic terminals in the nucleus accumbens and frontal cortex, the chemical signal is normally turned off by reabsorption of dopamine back into the synaptic terminal. This is accomplished by specialized proteins called dopamine **transporters**. It turns out that one of the primary ways cocaine acts on neurons is to block the activity of the dopamine transporter. This has the effect of inhibiting the reabsorption of dopamine back into the synaptic terminal, thereby greatly prolonging the ability of dopamine to stimulate receiving neurons. It is this continued stimulation of receiving neurons in the nucleus accumbens and frontal cortex by dopamine that is believed to result in the euphoric high produced by crack cocaine.

TOLERANCE—CHASING THAT FIRST HIGH

The repeated use of cocaine in any form results in a phenomenon called "**tolerance**." Tolerance occurs when the body and brain adjust to the continued presence of cocaine in the body, making it more resistant to the effects of the drug. For example, let's say the first time a person (we will call him "John") tries crack he smokes a crack rock weighing about 100 milligrams and obtains the most intense high of his life. Once the high wears off, John is left feeling irritable, anxious, and depressed. The memory of how good he felt after he smoked crack is still fresh in his mind, however, and he wants to try it again. So he buys some more crack and smokes another rock about the same size as the first. This time, however, the high he achieves, while still intense, isn't as good as the first time. So John goes out and buys a bigger bag of crack, and the next time he tries smoking a rock that is a little bit bigger, weighing 150 milligrams. This time he gets a really intense high, but soon afterward he finds himself feeling somewhat paranoid about being caught by the police, which ruins the experience of the high. So, as John ends up chasing that initial high he found to be so intensely euphoric the first time he smoked crack, he spirals into crack addiction, eventually spending all his money on crack rather than paying his bills or having enough money for food. John's body has begun to adapt to the repeated presence of cocaine in his brain, and has built a biological "barrier" against obtaining the intensity of that first high.

In summary, the highly addictive nature of crack cocaine is primarily believed to be a result of its rapid entry into the brain after smoking, and of the intense and immediate euphoria that it produces by acting within the brain's pleasure centers. Also, tolerance to the euphoric effects of crack can cause the user to continually pursue taking more and more of the drug in an attempt to obtain that first high he or she found so pleasurable.

3

History of Crack Cocaine

Marilyn remembers first hearing references to crack cocaine in the middle of her junior year of high school in early 1986. She started to hear jokes and people poking fun at others when someone did something outrageously funny or silly, with sayings like "What are you, on crack?" Other times she would hear someone refer to a teacher who was trying to teach something hard to understand as having been "hitting the crack pipe." At first she had no idea what the crack comments were in reference to until she saw a news story on the crack "epidemic," which showed video clips of people lighting these little white rocks made of cocaine and smoking the fumes through a glass pipe. Now she understood what they were talking about. Marilyn was a good student and wasn't friends with people who were into hard drugs like cocaine.

Then one evening when she and her friends were having a few beers at Marilyn's house before a high school dance (her parents had gone out to dinner), Marilyn's friend Alicia reached into her purse and pulled out a glass pipe and a plastic bag containing what looked from a distance to be little white pebbles. "Anyone want to try a little rock?" her friend suggested. Marilyn and the rest of her friends said in collective astonishment: "Are you CRAZY?!?!?"

"I've heard that stuff is dangerously addictive," Marilyn said, and her other friends agreed.

"Don't believe everything you hear," replied Alicia. "Come on. Don't be wimps."

"No way!" Marilyn and her friends exclaimed.

"Suit yourself, ladies," Alicia sniffed as she went outside to smoke by herself. She came back glassy-eyed and high as a kite. "I'm in heaven," Alicia beamed. "Let's go to the dance!"

They all went to the dance, but in the weeks and months that followed, Alicia seemed to drift away from her close-knit group of friends and eventually became somewhat of a loner and seemed depressed all the time. Eventually Alicia's parents pulled her out of Marilyn's high school and sent her to a different school across town that catered to kids with drug or family problems. The stone had gotten the best of Alicia until she eventually was referred to a cocaine-addiction treatment facility.

When compared to drugs like opium, tobacco, and alcohol, crack cocaine is relatively new. It first appeared on the drug scene in the mid-1980s, and thus has only been around for a little more than two decades. Before discussing how crack cocaine came to be, however, it is important to know a bit about the general history of cocaine.

BRIEF HISTORY OF COCAINE

The use of cocaine, which comes from the coca plant—*Erythroxylum coca*—that grows in South America, dates back at least a thousand years. Drawings of the coca plant have been found on artifacts such as pottery that date back to almost A.D. 1000.[8] It is believed that the Incan people of Peru chewed coca leaves for their stimulant effects. When South America was invaded by the Spanish Conquistadors in the sixteenth century, however, the conquerors imposed an oppressive set of rules on the Incan way of life, and use of the drug decreased. When the Spanish rulers found that allowing their Native South American slaves to chew coca leaves made them more energetic and hardworking and less tired and hungry, however, the drug's popularity re-emerged. In the sixteenth century, coca leaves made their way back to the homeland of the Spaniards and its use spread to many countries in Europe.

Figure 3.1   Dr. Sigmund Freud (1856-1939) is believed to have used cocaine to combat his depression. In the nineteenth century, cocaine was used for many medical purposes. *(© Getty Images.)*

In 1855, a German chemist named Friedrich Gaedke isolated the primary **psychoactive** ingredient from the coca leaf and called it "Erythroxyline." In 1860, chemist Albert Niemann further isolated this psychoactive ingredient to almost 100 percent purity and called it "cocaine." By comparison, however, coca leaves themselves only contain about 0.1 percent to 0.9 percent cocaine by weight. Identification and purification of the main stimulant ingredient of the coca leaf subsequently allowed for it to be marketed to the rest of the world in stimulating and healthful drinks such as the cocaine-containing wine Vin Mariani or even the soft drink Coca-Cola. Some famous historical figures who were reported to be users of cocaine include William Shakespeare, U.S. President William McKinley, Pope Leo XVII, and inventor Thomas Edison.

Medicinal uses of cocaine were also discovered in the nineteenth century. People found that cocaine acted as a potent anesthetic (numbing) agent, so it was used as a local anesthetic for various surgical procedures such as ear, nose, eye, and throat surgery. Cocaine was also once marketed as a cure for toothaches. Because cocaine causes blood vessels to constrict, some people advocated the use of cocaine to help control bleeding and for heart ailments such as irregular heartbeats. Cocaine was administered to German soldiers in World War II to enhance their endurance in physical tasks and military maneuvers.

One medical-cocaine advocate was the noted psychiatrist Dr. Sigmund Freud, who reportedly took cocaine daily in order to combat his own depression and indigestion.[9,10] After becoming enamored with the europhia that cocaine produced, Freud eventually advocated the use of cocaine as a mental stimulant, treatment for digestive disorders, a treatment for asthma, an aphrodisiac, a local anesthetic, and even as a treatment for morphine addiction and alcoholism. These recommended uses of cocaine were published in his monograph *Über Coca*. This last recommendation brought great criticism from his fellow psychiatrists, since they felt treating morphine addiction or alcoholism with cocaine was simply replacing one addiction with another.

By the early 1900s, recreational use of cocaine had become widespread. Cocaine was being sold in wines, cola drinks, chocolate candies, and toothache remedies, and could even

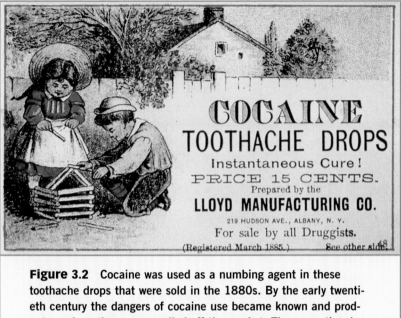

Figure 3.2 Cocaine was used as a numbing agent in these toothache drops that were sold in the 1880s. By the early twentieth century the dangers of cocaine use became known and products such as these were pulled off the market. The recreational use of cocaine became illegal in 1914 with the passage of the Harrison Narcotic Act *(© CORBIS.)*

be purchased in department stores. The ill effects of taking cocaine for recreational purposes, however, were starting to be recognized. Such ill effects included tremors, hallucinations, heart attacks and **strokes**, addiction, and even death. In 1912 the U.S. government reported about 5,000 deaths as a result of cocaine use. As a result, the Harrison Narcotic Act was passed in 1914, which was primarily aimed at controlling the sale and distribution of narcotics such as morphine and opium, but also prohibited the use of cocaine except for medical use as a local anesthetic, and imposed severe penalties for possessing or distributing cocaine. As a result of the Harrison Act, cocaine use for recreational purposes was driven into the underground black market, along with narcotics such as heroin. As a result, people who persisted in their efforts to take cocaine were classified as criminals, as were the people who continued to import or sell cocaine for such uses. In the 1930s, however, the synthesis of amphetamines was first accomplished, and these new stimulants became the drug of choice for several decades, causing the use of cocaine to decline.

In 1970 the U.S. government passed the Controlled Substances Act, which classified all drugs into one of five categories, or **schedules** (see Appendix 1), according to how medically useful, safe, and potentially addictive they are. Today cocaine is classified as a Schedule II controlled substance, because although it has a high potential for addiction, it is still medically useful as a local anesthetic agents in certain surgical procedures, such as those on the eye. Punishment for possession of cocaine varies by state in the United States, ranging from as little as a misdemeanor charge with a fine for possession of a small amount of cocaine, to sentencing of 5 to 10 years in prison for possession of large amounts of cocaine, especially if the cocaine is intended to be distributed and sold.

... AND ALONG CAME CRACK

It is not known precisely when crack cocaine was first produced, or who invented it, but crack cocaine first gained the attention of the media in the mid-1980s. In November 1984, the *Los Angeles Times* published a small story on local "rock houses" selling pellets of cocaine for as little as $25. The term *crack*, however, was not actually used in this story. About a year later, *New York Times* journalist Donna Boundy published a story on a drug-abuse treatment program in the New York area where several teenagers had sought treatment for addiction to a new form of cocaine called "crack" for its rock-like appearance. (The article also referred to crack as a freebase and concentrated form of cocaine, which is actually not the case, since crack cocaine is not necessarily more concentrated—i.e., more cocaine molecules per milligram—than traditional powdered cocaine.)

Within less than a year of the appearance of Boundy's article in the *New York Times*, the major mainstream news media publications in the United States, such as *Time, Newsweek,* and *U.S.*

News and World Report magazines, along with major metropolitan newspapers, including the *Los Angeles Times* and *Miami Herald*, had published more than 1,000 stories on crack cocaine. Soon to follow were TV documentaries such as "48 Hours on Crack Street" on CBS and "Cocaine Country" on NBC.

THE CRACK EPIDEMIC: FACT OR MEDIA MYTH?

During the sharp rise in the number of stories in the media about crack cocaine in the mid-1980s, journalists began referring to the use and spread of crack cocaine across the United States as a "plague," "epidemic," or "crisis," reporting that crack use was "flooding America" and had become the number one "drug of choice." This terminology gave the American public the impression that crack use had invaded every city and its use was commonplace among all drug users. Due to this media hype, the U.S. Drug Enforcement Administration (DEA) was compelled to compile and release an official report on the status of crack in America in 1986.[11] In this report, although admitting that crack was indeed being manufactured, sold, and smoked in major metropolitan areas such as Los Angeles; Denver; Atlanta; Washington, D.C.; Seattle; Miami; Detroit; and Houston; the DEA stated that powdered cocaine was still the predominant form of cocaine being used. It further stated that snorting was still the most common route of administration for cocaine. This DEA report also stated that there had been a distortion in the public's opinion on the extent of crack use, and that the crack problem was secondary to that of powdered cocaine. Despite this report, newspapers, TV networks, and magazines continued to publish and broadcast a high volume of stories related to crack cocaine for several years. The hype of the crack epidemic eventually faded from focus of the media in the early 1990s.

So was the crack "epidemic" nothing more than a catchphrase stirred up by the news media? There are many people who would argue in hindsight that the crack scare was overblown by both the media and various political figures, including President Ronald

Reagan and his wife Nancy. Nevertheless, the fact remains that today crack can be found in many metropolitan areas as well as surrounding suburban regions across the country, and its addiction potential is still a tremendous threat to anyone who might come into contact with it.

IMPORTATION OF COCAINE INTO THE UNITED STATES AND ITS SPREAD TO THE SUBURBS

Powdered cocaine is smuggled into the United States from South American countries such as Colombia, Peru, and Bolivia via two primary routes: the Mexico-Central America corridor (which accounts for approximately 72 percent of cocaine in the U.S.), and the Caribbean corridor (which accounts for approximately 26 percent of cocaine in the U.S.).[12] Through these corridors, cocaine is smuggled northward from country to country until it eventually reaches the United States. Only about 2 percent of cocaine in the United States is smuggled directly from South American countries. Once inside the United States, cocaine is primarily distributed to inner-city neighborhoods in large metropolitan areas such as New York, Los Angeles, and Chicago. It is here that powdered cocaine is converted into crack cocaine.

When crack cocaine first emerged as a new, cheaper, and powerfully addictive form of cocaine in the mid-1980s, its distribution, sale, and use was primarily confined to the inner-city neighborhoods where it first arrived in the United States. By the late 1980s, however, crack use had spread to surrounding suburban areas, and its use had increased among affluent and middle-income Americans.[13] Doctors, lawyers, bankers, and even homemakers were becoming exposed and addicted to crack. Crack was no longer an inner-city problem. It now gripped middle- and upper-income areas with the same destructive nature as in ghettos and slums of major cities in the United States.

THE "WAR ON DRUGS"

Politicians are often known to declare "war" on certain problems in society. These "wars" are slogans that usually represent a strong and focused effort on the part of the U.S. government to combat a problem that is perceived as a

Figure 3.3 Ronald Reagan is the president most often associated with the War on Drugs, however, this "war" predated Reagan's presidency. *(© Getty Images)*

significant threat to the well-being of society. The use of the term war is primarily aimed at implying a state of emergency and unified governmental approach at solving the problem. In the 1960s, President Lyndon Johnson declared a "War on Poverty," and following the September 11, 2001, terrorist attacks on the United States, President George W. Bush declared a "War on Terror." Prior to these "wars," however, the U.S. government declared a "War on Drugs." Although the War on Drugs is usually associated with the Reagan administration, the term was coined prior to Reagan's presidency and the war itself dates back more than a century. Some examples of early large-scale attempts by the U.S. government at curbing drug use, sale, manufacturing, and trafficking included:

- the Opium Wars of the nineteenth century, when the United States was attempting to stem the flow of opium from China to the United States; this led to the governments of the United States and China eventually signing an agreement in 1880 prohibiting the sale and trafficking of opium to the United States

- the Harrison Narcotic Act in 1914, which regulated the production and distribution narcotics as well as cocaine

- the Prohibition Era of 1919–1933, when the manufacture, sale, and use of alcohol was prohibited

- the Marijuana Tax Act of 1937, which added a $1 tax to the distribution of marijuana in an effort to curb the use of the drug

- the Controlled Substances Act of 1970, which classified all psychoactive substances into various categories or "schedules," based on their medical usefulness as well as their potential to produce addiction and dependence

Despite these earlier efforts, the official "War on Drugs" was actually started under President Richard Nixon when at a news conference on June 17, 1971, he declared illegal drugs

Figure 3.4 President Richard M. Nixon declared a "War on Drugs" in the early 1970s. Here he is being presented with a report on the doubling of drug arrests in two years since his War on Drugs campaign started. *(© Bettmann/CORBIS.)*

to be "public enemy number one" in the United States. The Nixon administration enacted the 1970 Controlled Substances Act and assigned its enforcement to the Bureau of Narcotics and Dangerous Drugs, which would later become the Drug Enforcement Administration. In the 1980s, President Ronald Reagan and his wife would add substantial vigor to the War on Drugs with many public statements and efforts to control drug use and trafficking on national and international levels. One of these efforts was Nancy Reagan's "Just Say No" prevention campaign, which was aimed at teaching children and teenagers to help stop the problem of drug addiction by simply turning away from drugs and their users and dealers. The Reagan administration also enacted the Anti-Drug Abuse Act of 1988, the intent of which was to establish a drug-free America. A key provision of this act was the formation of the Office of National Drug

Control Policy (ONDCP) to set priorities, implement a national strategy, and certify federal drug-control budgets. The director of this office is often dubbed the nation's **drug czar**.

The War on Drugs is not without its critics, however. Many economists and government policy analysts view the War on Drugs as a massive failure. For example, in 2005, the U.S. government budgeted more than $14 billion for drug control and prevention, including $2 billion for drug-use prevention and prevention research, $5 billion for recovery and treatment programs and research, and $7 billion for disrupting drug manufacturing, trafficking, and sale.[14] Despite these budget figures, it is estimated that only approximately one third of cocaine being smuggled into the U.S. is actually intercepted.[15]

Meanwhile, some critics have accused the U.S. government of political hypocrisy in its War on Drugs. For example, despite a public stance against drug use and trafficking, the U.S. government during the 1980s—while training and arming the Contra rebels of Nicaragua to help them fight against their then-communist government—funded the Contras' training by allowing the shipment of large quantities of cocaine into the United States using government-owned aircraft and military facilities.[16] So, while urging people to say "no" to drugs, the U.S. government was actually illegally paying for wars in other countries by facilitating the import of cocaine into the United States.

4

Demographics of Crack Use

In a 1989 article in the New York Times, *writer Andrew Malcolm interviewed several middle- to upper-class people whose lives were destroyed by addiction to crack, highlighting the drug's spread outside of the inner city. One of these individuals—Hal, a successful investment banker—said he had experimented with marijuana, amphetamines, and powdered cocaine in high school and college. Eventually Hal tried smoking crack and was hooked in a short amount of time. "I can't tell you how high crack made me feel . . . or how frightened of the low (crash) I was. I'd smoke even when my left arm went numb and I got severe chest pains." Eventually, Hal was fired from his investment banking job that paid him $300,000 a year. After being fired, Hal borrowed money from friends or even banks to support his crack habit. Eventually a friend of Hal's (who happened to be a former crack addict) talked him into committing himself to a psychiatric hospital for treatment. Two days later, Hal checked himself out of the hospital and went on a two-day binge of smoking more than $5,000 worth of crack. Hal eventually was able to quit crack with the help of a substance-abuse treatment professional. Hal's story is an example of the powerful addictive nature of crack, and how the "rock" knows no socioeconomic boundaries. It can hook anyone.*

TRENDS IN THE USE OF CRACK

As discussed in earlier chapters, the use of crack cocaine did not surface until the mid-1980s. Thus, compared to the use of other drugs, there is a relatively small amount of data collected over the past two decades regarding crack use. Nonetheless, one large-scale government study was the 2002–2003 National Survey on Drug Use and Health (NSDUH),[17] which surveyed more than 130,000 people age 12 or older on whether they had used cocaine (in any form) in the previous month or year. The results showed that 0.6 percent of the respondents, which translates to an estimated 1.5 million people in the United States, had used crack cocaine in the previous year. Also, 0.2 percent of the respondents (which translates to an estimated 586,000 people in the United States) had used crack cocaine in the previous month.

Prior to the appearance of crack cocaine in the mid-1980s, the use of cocaine was slowly but steadily rising, as was the incidence of cocaine-related emergencies such as heart attacks, strokes, overdoses, and deaths. When crack cocaine was introduced, however, the number of cocaine-related emergency room (ER) visits and cocaine-related deaths increased by more than five times that of previous years.[18] The number of cocaine-related ER visits and deaths did not taper off until approximately 1989–1990.

More recently, however, the use of crack appears to be diminishing slowly, while the use of powdered (snorted or inhaled) cocaine appears to be regaining some popularity. For example, the percentage of people admitted to drug treatment facilities for problems related to crack (i.e., smoked) cocaine in 1995 was 79 percent, while this figure was only 14 percent during the same year for people using inhaled (i.e., snorted) cocaine. In contrast, in 2005, the percentage of people admitted who were smoking crack had fallen to 73 percent, while the percentage of people admitted who were snorting cocaine had risen to 22 percent.[19] These data suggest that, at least in terms of people who seek treatment for cocaine addiction, there is a trend for decreasing usage of crack cocaine and an increase in usage of snorted cocaine. This is the exact opposite of what happened in the mid-1980s. From these data, however, it is still obvious that

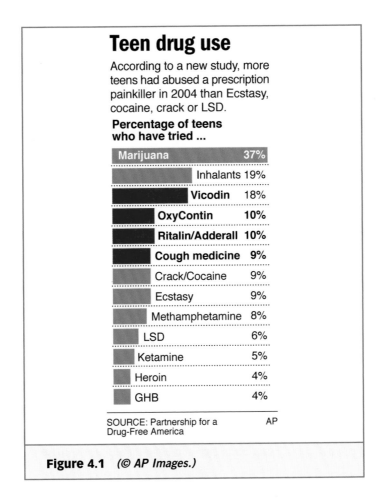

Figure 4.1 *(© AP Images.)*

crack users represent the majority of cocaine addicts who enter treatment facilities.

TRENDS IN THE AGE OF CRACK USERS

Due to its low cost and ease of availability, crack has generally appealed to younger people of the inner city. Over the past decade, however, there has been a trend for increased cocaine use among people who are slightly older. For example, the percentage of crack users being admitted to cocaine-treatment facilities in the age range of 18 to 25 decreased from

15 percent to 9 percent from 1995 to 2005. Similarly, the percentage of crack users in the age range of 26 to 34 being admitted to treatment facilities decreased by more than half, from 47 percent to 22 percent, in the same time period. The percentage of crack users between the ages of 35 and 49, however, increased from 35 percent to 59 percent, and even the percentage of crack users older than 50 increased from 5 percent to 9 percent from 1995 to 2005. These figures suggest that crack use is finding increasing popularity in older people—people who are not normally associated with use

CRACK USE BY SENIOR CITIZENS?

Despite the widely held belief that crack use and addiction primarily afflicts younger people, there are case reports of senior citizens with crack habits. A 2007 report from Great Britain[20] described an elderly man who became addicted to crack. This man (the authors of the report called him "Mr. A") at age 68 was introduced to powdered cocaine by a sex worker to boost his sexual performance. By age 70, Mr. A started using crack and developed a very expensive crack habit. Soon he had became estranged and divorced from his wife due to his crack addiction, moved into a separate house from which he was later evicted, and accumulated a significant amount of debt to his friends and family members. In addition to his personal relationship problems, Mr. A's mental health started to unravel, and he became deeply depressed and had thoughts of suicide. Recognizing his numerous serious problems, his family members had him committed to an inpatient psychiatric clinic and eventually to a drug rehabilitation program. After months of treatment, Mr. A's mental health and family relationships began to improve, and he was able to abstain from using crack, although occasionally he still suffered episodes of relapse. This case scenario, although less common, demonstrates the ability of crack to pull people of any age into addiction to this drug.

of hard drugs such as crack. It is likely, however, that many people who were smoking crack when it first came out in the 1980s are still smoking it today while advancing into older age groups, which may explain the increase in frequency of use of crack by people above the age of 50.

CRACK USE, GENDER, RACE, AND ETHNICITY

Because crack evolved in the poverty-stricken inner-city neighborhoods of major metropolitan areas in which there were high concentrations of Latinos and African Americans, the use of crack has often been perceived as a "Hispanic" or "black" problem. According to the 2006 NSDUH study,[21] however, the percentage of people who reported having used crack at least once in the past year, sorted according to ethnic background, were as follows

Caucasian	0.5 percent
Black/African American	1.3 percent
American Indian/Alaskan Native	3.0 percent
Native Hawaiian/Other Pacific Islander	0.5 percent
Asian	0.2 percent
Latino	0.7 percent
Multiracial	0.5 percent

Thus, this recent survey data shows that of all the different ethnicities that use crack (at least those that were surveyed), American Indian and/or Alaskan Natives appear to be the most frequent users, not Latinos or African Americans.

Stereotypes also often tend to portray males are being more likely to be crack users than females. This actually appears to be the case, however, since this same 2006 survey reported that approximately 70 percent of crack users were male, while only 30 percent were female. There are a number of possible explanations for this gender difference in crack use. One is that, historically, society has been more willing to permit men to take intoxicating substances than women, often portraying men as risk-taking or creative yet troubled; drug-using women are often stigmatized as being sexually promiscuous, and are ostracized due to the potential hazardous effects that taking drugs has on a developing fetus, should she become pregnant.[22]

GEOGRAPHIC TRENDS IN CRACK USE

The use of crack tends to be concentrated in large metropolitan areas (i.e., cities with populations more than one million residents). Cities including Atlanta, Phoenix, San Francisco, Los Angeles, St. Louis, Miami, Philadelphia, New York City, Washington, Denver, Minneapolis, Detroit, New Orleans, and Boston all have high frequencies of crack use, with about 3.6 percent of each city's inhabitants reporting the use of crack at least once in his or her lifetime. Smaller metropolitan areas (i.e., cities with between 250,000 and one million residents) have similar rates of crack use. Very rural, small-town areas tend to have the lowest frequency of crack use (i.e., an average of about 2.3 percent of their inhabitants reporting having used crack at least once in their lifetime).

CRACK USE AND EMPLOYMENT

According to a 2007 report by the Drug and Alcohol Services Information System, the highest percentage of people who use crack tend to be unemployed or unable to work, accounting for more than 80 percent of all crack users. This survey also indicated that only 5 percent of people with part-time jobs use crack, while 12 percent of people with full-time jobs use crack. Researchers often refer to crack users who have full-time jobs as "hidden" users,[23] since they rarely participate in research studies or surveys because they have more to risk (such as losing their jobs) if their crack habits were exposed to their employers. (Recall Hal's story from the start of this chapter). Because the crack high wears off with in an hour or two, however, people with full-time jobs must go through extra efforts to hide their crack habit, perhaps sneaking into the parking lot or restroom many times throughout the day, increasing their risk of getting caught.

As mentioned earlier, crack is a relatively inexpensive way to use cocaine since buying a few rocks can cost as little as $10. Heavy crack users may use several rocks per day, costing them as much as $350 a week (or $18,000 a year) to support their habit,[24] depending on the current pricing of crack cocaine. So if crack users are largely unemployed, how do they support their drug habits? Most get their money from friends, family members, or other acquaintances, but also often through committing crimes such as burglary or prostitution, or even as drug dealers.[25,26] These topics are covered in detail in the following chapter.

5

Crack, Crime, and Violence

Jimmy has been hooked on crack for a few months and has been able to hold down his job at a grocery as a stock clerk, taking frequent breaks out at the loading dock to hit the pipe every few hours. One day, however, his supervisor caught him lighting up, and Jimmy lost his job immediately. Not having much in his savings account, Jimmy quickly ran out of cash to support his crack habit. For a few weeks he borrowed money from friends, but they soon learned what he was up to and eventually refused to lend any more money. Desperate to support his habit, Jimmy started begging on street corners of downtown Los Angeles for spare change, but this only netted him about $20 a day, which wasn't enough to cover his $100-a-day habit. So Jimmy started pickpocketing as he walked the streets of downtown L.A. On his second day of this new source of income, he pickpocketed the wrong person, who chased Jimmy down and beat him severely. Jimmy began to grow increasingly agitated over his financial situation, and his cravings for crack grew even stronger as he tried to get back to the ability to afford to smoke five rocks a day. So one day he borrowed his dealer's pistol and robbed several convenience stores, nabbing about $2,000 in cash. Soon this money was gone, spent entirely on crack, and he went on another robbery spree, this time hitting a few banks in the area with the hopes of landing a bigger payload. At one of the banks, Jimmy was caught on surveillance videotape and was arrested the next day for armed robbery. Jimmy now sits in a 6-by-8-foot jail cell awaiting trial, which could lead to 10 years' imprisonment.

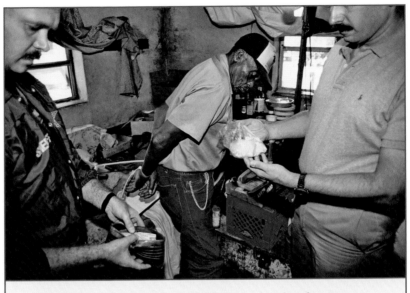

Figure 5.1 The rise of crack led to a rise in crime for many areas in the United States. This Florida man is being arrested for dealing crack. (© *Steve Starr/CORBIS.*)

There is no doubt that the introduction of crack has had a tremendous impact on society. Laws have been enacted to counter its use, manufacture, and sale; the War on Drugs has taken a tremendous economic toll on society, not to mention the loss of economic productivity from the crack users themselves. Crack destroys families and relationships; and many health problems are a direct result of crack use. The one issue that seems to draw the most public concern, however, is the relationship between crack, crime, and violence.

Since its introduction to society in the mid-1980s, there has been a strong public perception that crack use is highly associated with criminal behavior. There are reports of gang "turf wars" over which inner-city gang has control over selling crack in a particular neighborhood. Crack users often steal valuables from homes or stores in order to support their habit. Crack users are often perceived as willing to do anything (even commit murder) in order to score that next batch of rock. Is there hard evidence to support the public perception that crack users are more likely to be violent or commit crimes than any other type of drug user?

STATISTICAL CORRELATIONS

One way researchers have examined the relationship between crack and crime is by questioning jail and prison inmates on their use of drugs in or around the time of the crime they committed; sometimes, samples of blood or urine are given for testing for the presence of cocaine **metabolites**. One such project that employs this method is the Arrestee Drug Abuse Monitoring (ADAM) program, formerly known as the Drug Use Forecasting (DUF) program. In a 1997 report from this program, 20 percent of arrestees had used crack cocaine during the month before the commission of the particular crime for which they were arrested, but only 9 percent of these individuals were using crack at the actual time the crime was committed.[27] By 2002, this latter statistic has risen slightly to 11 percent.[28] Clearly, these percentages indicate that actual use of crack is not highly associated with criminal behavior, but in the period surrounding the crime (perhaps when the crack user was looking for ways to obtain money to buy crack), criminal behavior may increase. Other studies have confirmed a strong relationship between the use of crack and engagement in criminal behavior such as theft and burglary, crimes that are primarily committed in order to obtain money to buy crack.[29,30] Oftentimes, crack users will engage in sexual activities in return for obtaining crack.[31,32] For teenagers, crack use often leads to truancy (skipping school). Of course, possession, selling, and trafficking of crack are also crimes, which increases the likelihood that a crack user will have a criminal record.

CRACK AND VIOLENT CRIME

Use of crack cocaine is not only associated with nonviolent crimes like theft and drug possession, but there are a significant number

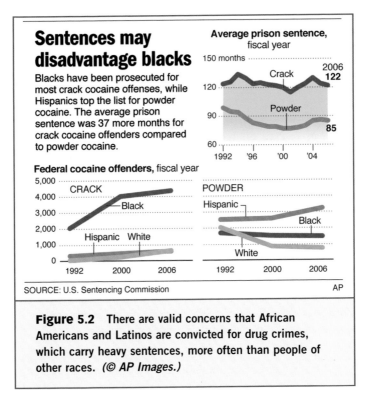

Sentences may disadvantage blacks

Blacks have been prosecuted for most crack cocaine offenses, while Hispanics top the list for powder cocaine. The average prison sentence was 37 more months for crack cocaine offenders compared to powder cocaine.

Average prison sentence, fiscal year

Crack 2006 122

Powder 85

Federal cocaine offenders, fiscal year

CRACK — Black, Hispanic, White

POWDER — Hispanic, Black, White

SOURCE: U.S. Sentencing Commission   AP

Figure 5.2   There are valid concerns that African Americans and Latinos are convicted for drug crimes, which carry heavy sentences, more often than people of other races. *(© AP Images.)*

of studies suggesting a relationship between crack and violent crime.[33] This may be the case for several reasons, as hypothesized by researchers during the first year of the crack "epidemic."[34]

The first reason has to do with the psychopharmacological effects of crack cocaine. Crack users may feel emboldened by the euphoria of the cocaine high, and thus engage in more risky behavior. As a crack high wears off, the user begins to "crash," experiencing symptoms such as fatigue, depression, irritability, and insomnia. This often leads the crack user to try to relieve these **acute** withdrawal symptoms by smoking more crack. As a result, crack users usually tend to go on crack **binges**, where the user smokes crack once every several hours for a period of up to several days. When the crack user finally runs out of crack, money, or is completely exhausted, a more intense period of withdrawal may begin, often accompanied by **paranoia** and **psychosis** (a loss of touch with reality), which may cause the crack user to behave in irrational and violent ways.

The second reason has to do with what has been termed **economic compulsion**. Because of the highly addictive nature

CRACK GETS POLITICAL—THE STORY OF MARION BARRY

The story of Marion Barry is an exceptional example of how crack use transcends all socioeconomic boundaries. Marion Shepilov Barry Jr., born in 1936 in Itta Bena, Mississippi, was elected to the city council of Washington, D.C., in 1974, and elected as mayor in 1978. He initially served three consecutive four-year terms as mayor. On January 18, 1990, however, Barry was arrested as part of a sting operation conducted by the Washington, D.C., police and FBI, along with the help of Barry's girlfriend Hazel "Rasheeda" Moore, a police informant. Barry was caught on police surveillance videotape in a hotel room smoking crack, and was charged with three felony counts of perjury, 10 counts of misdemeanor drug possession, and one misdemeanor count of conspiracy to possess cocaine. Barry, however, ended up being convicted of only a single charge: misdemeanor possession of cocaine from an incident in November 1989, two months prior to the videotaped sting operation. Barry was sentenced in October 1990 to a six-month term in a federal prison, and was forced to step down as mayor of Washington.

The story does not end there. After being released from prison, Barry was successful in obtaining a city council seat in 1992 and eventually elected again as mayor of Washington in 1994, where he served another full four-year term. His campaign slogan was "He May Not Be Perfect, But He's Perfect for D.C." Many people view Barry's second stint as mayor as a symbol for public forgiveness. His entanglements with the law have continued, however, as he pleaded guilty in 2005 for of crack, a crack user's continued use of the drug plunges him or her deeper and deeper into dependency on the drug. Within this downward spiral into the depths of crack addiction, the crack user's willingness to use money obtained legally to support his or her crack habit may begin to dissipate, causing the

Figure 5.3   Marion Barry. (© *Jeffrey Markowitz/Sygma/ CORBIS.*)

failing to pay federal and local taxes (incidentally, at a mandatory drug test at a 2005 court appearance, Barry tested positive for cocaine and marijuana use). In September 2006, Barry was charged with driving under the influence, but he was acquitted in June 2007.

crack addict to rely increasingly on illegal ways of obtaining money for crack. While theft of valuables from a home or place of business may be nonviolent, many times the crime may turn violent (e.g., armed robbery, assault, perhaps even murder) if the addict faces opposition or confrontation from others in the process of obtaining the means to purchase more crack. This is especially true if the crack addict is extremely desperate or impulsive about doing anything to get the money for the next hit, regardless of the consequences. Paranoia and irritability, which is often a result from chronic crack use, can cause people to do irrational and violent things in order to support their drug habit.

One final reason that crack use is often associated with violence is the violent nature of the crack subculture, which has been called the **systemic model**. Typically, people involved in the crack business are also involved in other criminal activities. Guns, illegal sexual activity, theft, and violence are part of everyday life in the crack world, and this lifestyle is often reinforced by the glorification of sex and crime by various facets of the entertainment industry. There are also violent gang turf wars over crack distribution "rights" in certain neighborhoods. Police informants, if caught by drug dealers, are often murdered. People who sell fake drugs or those who have outstanding drug debts are often victims of assault or murder. As a result, violence becomes a way of life for the crack addict. In other words, it comes with the territory. Research has shown, however, that the vast majority of crack-related crimes are perpetrated between drug dealers or between dealers and users. This sets up a vicious cycle, whereby crime-ridden neighborhoods where crack is predominantly sold become inhabited by drug dealers and users, who perpetuate the violence within the inner-city community by committing drug-related crimes against each other.

IS THERE A CAUSAL RELATIONSHIP BETWEEN CRACK AND CRIME?

There is no doubt that crack use is associated with higher levels of criminal behavior than using "softer" drugs like cigarettes. Does this mean that crack *causes* one to become a criminal, particularly a violent criminal? The answer is likely no. Longitudinal studies (i.e., studies of individuals over a large portion of their lifetime) have shown that criminal behavior in a person often emerges prior to their first use of crack.[35] A crack user most often commits crime like theft, robbery, or prostitution several years prior to the first use of crack. Because repeated smoking of crack can cause symptoms of psychosis and paranoia, desperation over how to support the crack habit, induction into the violent crack subculture, and a deterioration of interpersonal relationships, the drug itself seems to compound any pre-existing disposition toward engaging in criminal behavior. In this way crack appears to initiate a vicious cycle that, once started, can send the user on a violent road to ruin.

6

Psychological and Medical Consequences of Crack Use

Raul liked to smoke crack every weekend with several of his friends. They would often smoke at an abandoned warehouse less than a mile from where Raul lived. One weekend, after "scoring" a big purchase of $40 worth of crack, Raul and three of his friends met at their usual spot with the intent of getting "higher than they ever had before." Raul started first and smoked almost an entire rock before passing the pipe along to his friend. While sitting in the corner feeling his high come on, he started to sweat and feel a pain in his chest. Within another minute the chest pain was excruciating and his whole left arm went numb. He cried out in pain but his friends paid him no attention, as they were too busy getting their turn at the pipe. Raul then blacked out, and his heart stopped. By the time his friends finished their hits on the crack pipe, they were too wasted to even notice Raul lying unconscious in the corner.

When they finally came down from their high an hour later, they tried to wake Raul but his face was pale and he was not breathing. Instead of calling 911 for help, Raul's friends were stricken with fear that they might get caught with what was left of the crack cocaine when the police arrived, so they ran. It wasn't until two days later that Raul's body was found by a homeless man who frequented the abandoned warehouse for shelter. The homeless person flagged down a police car, told them that there was a body lying in the warehouse, and the police radioed for the coroner's van. An autopsy showed that Raul died of a massive heart attack, and that he had levels of cocaine in his bloodstream that were twice what was normally found in crack addicts shortly after smoking.

PSYCHOLOGICAL PROBLEMS

Cocaine produces some acute (rapid onset with a short duration) psychological effects such as poor judgment and **delirium**. Repeated and chronic use of crack, however, leads to more serious psychological problems. Crack users often go on binges, taking the drug repeatedly for days at a time. When the user finally runs out of crack or money, he or she may "crash" or go into withdrawal and begin to have feelings of irritability, anxiety, restlessness, depression, inability to experience pleasure (**anhedonia**), and insomnia. While heavy users of powdered cocaine can also experience these withdrawal symptoms, crack users are more likely to experience symptoms of psychosis. Such psychotic symptoms may include extreme paranoia, hallucinations, or **delusions of grandeur**. Another severe symptom of the crash following binging on crack is the feeling that bugs are crawling on or under one's skin (**tactile hallucinations**). These feelings may be so severe or seem so overwhelmingly real that the person may actually pick pieces of their skin off of their body.

MEDICAL PROBLEMS

The degree to which an illegal drug is deemed dangerous is often judged by the number of times the use of that particular drug is mentioned in hospital emergency room visits. These statistics are collected and analyzed by a branch of the U.S. government known as the Drug Abuse Warning Network (DAWN). Statistics from this organization have shown that soon after the introduction of crack in the mid-1980s, the number of cocaine-related emergency-room visits began to skyrocket relative to other drugs, including heroin, morphine, marijuana, and methamphetamine.[36,37] Although it might be pure coincidence, many people attribute this dramatic rise in cocaine-related emergencies to the introduction of crack cocaine. While many of the health problems described in this chapter are common to all types of cocaine that is used, some of them are unique to crack.

CARDIOVASCULAR EFFECTS

Aside from their effects on the brain, cocaine and crack cause the most problems with the cardiovascular system,[38] which consists of the heart and blood vessels (arteries, veins, and capillaries). Cocaine has a "triple whammy" effect on the cardiovascular system. First, cocaine causes the release of adrenaline, which stimulates the heart to beat faster (called **tachycardia**). The normal resting heart rate of an adult is between 60 and 100 beats per minute. After taking cocaine, the heart rate may jump to 120 to 150 beats per minute, and this effect may last for an hour or two. Second, cocaine causes blood vessels to constrict, which increases blood pressure (also called **hypertension**). So, not only does the heart beat faster under the influence of cocaine, but it also has to force the blood through smaller blood vessels, which causes excess strain on the cells that line the blood vessel walls. Finally, cocaine causes specialized types of cells in the blood called **platelets**, which are normally involved in the clotting process, to clump together or "aggregate." This **platelet aggregation** has the effect of thickening the blood and making it more prone to clotting.

As a result of these effects that cocaine has on the cardio-vascular system, some very serious conditions are associated with cocaine use. These include **myocardial infarction** (heart attack), **dysrhythmia, cardiomyopathy**, and **aortic dissection**. All of these conditions can be life-threatening, and are the major cause of cocaine-related deaths.

NEUROLOGICAL EFFECTS

Crack also has ill effects on the function of the brain and central nervous system. As a result of platelet aggregation, clots can form in the blood vessels of the brain, blocking the blood supply and causing brain tissue and nerve cells to die from lack of oxygen. This is known as an **ischemic stroke**. On the other hand, the increased blood pressure caused by cocaine causes stressful wear and tear on the linings of the blood vessels in the brain, which may cause them to burst and cause what is called a cerebral hemorrhage. This type of stroke is called a **hemorrhagic stroke**. Both ischemic and hemorrhagic strokes can be caused by excessive cocaine use,[39] and result in severe damage to the brain. This damage to the brain causes the loss of certain basic functions controlled by the brain such as speech, vision, and movement. If the stroke is severe enough, death can result.

Another common neurological problem caused by cocaine is **seizures** (also called convulsions), where the muscles of the body contract involuntarily, causing the person to lose control over movement and fall to the floor, similar to a patient with severe epilepsy. Cocaine-induced seizures are likely a result of the drug causing overstimulation of the brain. As a result of this overstimulation, nerve cells in the part of the brain that controls the muscles of the body become overactive, resulting in repeated and involuntary contractions of muscles all over the body. Seizures are often accompanied by loss of consciousness.

One other ill effect of cocaine on the nervous system is the development of movement disorders (medically referred to as **choreas** or **dyskinesias**). Cocaine interacts with the neurotransmitter dopamine in the brain, as discussed in Chapter 2. In addition to an important role in the experience of pleasure, dopamine also plays a crucial role in controlling voluntary movements of the arms, legs, hands, feet, torso, head, and face. With chronic use, cocaine disrupts the normal functioning of

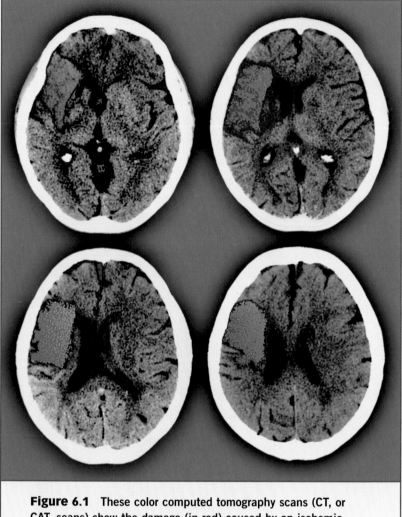

Figure 6.1 These color computed tomography scans (CT, or CAT, scans) show the damage (in red) caused by an ischemic stroke. (© Zephyr / Photo Researchers, Inc.)

dopamine in regions of the brain that control movements. The end result is the user experiences abnormal, repetitive, and involuntary movements such as shaking, foot-tapping, pacing, or rocking back and forth, twisting and writhing, teeth grinding, and facial grimaces. Some of the symptoms are similar to those found in Parkinson's disease. In addition, the abnormal movements induced by chronic cocaine use are often rhythmic in nature, and have been nicknamed **crack dancing**.[40]

PULMONARY EFFECTS

In people who snort or inject cocaine, problems with the pulmonary system (which includes the lungs and airways) are rare. Since crack users repeatedly take the drug by inhaling crack smoke, some pulmonary disturbances can develop. These include frequent coughs and shortness of breath due to irritation of the airways by crack-cocaine smoke. The upper airways, such as the throat and esophagus, can be burned and damaged by the heat of crack smoke. People with asthma who smoke crack can have their symptoms severely worsened, even to the point of death. Chronic crack users can develop **crack lung**, in which the tiny air sacs within the lung (called alveoli) where cocaine crosses into the bloodstream become irritated and scarred. These alveoli may even rupture, especially when crack users attempt to "hold in" the crack smoke for longer periods of time in an attempt to heighten the drug's psychological effects. Clots in the lungs (called **pulmonary embolisms**) can also result from use of crack cocaine.

CRACK AND THE SPREAD OF HIV AND AIDS

The spread of human immunodeficiency virus (HIV), which is the virus that causes acquired immunodeficiency syndrome (AIDS), is usually associated with intravenous drug users who share needles. Even though crack users take cocaine by smoking it, they still have a high incidence of HIV infection and AIDS. This is primarily because crack users often engage in risky sexual behaviors (such as having unprotected sex or engaging in prostitution to support a crack habit); crack users also may abuse other drugs besides crack (such as heroin, which is injected intravenously). In addition, sharing of crack pipes can spread HIV if one or more of the users has an open sore or wound in his or her mouth. Crack users often have

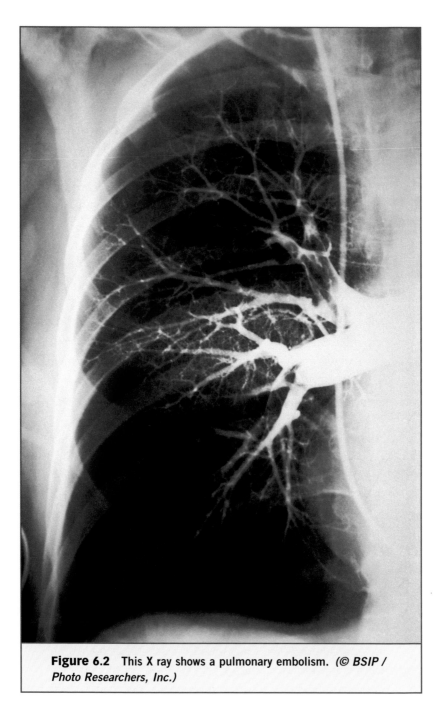

Figure 6.2   This X ray shows a pulmonary embolism. *(© BSIP / Photo Researchers, Inc.)*

burns or sores in their mouths because of overheating of the crack pipe, which causes damage to the tissue in the mouth when the crack is smoked.

CRACK BABIES

During the crack "epidemic" of the mid-1980s, the term **crack babies** was coined for babies who were born to crack-addicted mothers. These babies often had low birth weights and were undersized, and were more likely to be victims of sudden infant death syndrome (SIDS), where the infant dies in its sleep for no apparent reason. During the late 1980s and early 1990s, it was believed that repeated exposure of the fetus to crack caused the babies to sustain irreversible mental and physical damage, and it was thought that chances for the baby to have a normal life were close to zero. Fortunately, research over the past decade or so has shown that with the proper postnatal care, most babies born addicted to crack recover physically and have only limited deficits in psychological function, which include learning disabilities and attention difficulties.

OTHER ADVERSE EFFECTS

Cocaine is known to induce a syndrome called **rhabdomyolysis**, which is the abnormal breakdown of muscle tissue. This condition may be caused by cocaine by itself, or may be a result of the ability of cocaine to decrease appetite. Over time, rhabdomyolysis and decreased appetite may make crack users eventually become overly thin and emaciated. Rhabodomyolysis results in the excess accumulation of a muscle protein called myoglobin in the bloodstream, which can cause the kidneys to stop working properly (**renal failure**).

There are some ill effects from cocaine that are largely dependent on the route by which the drug is taken. People who snort cocaine regularly often develop inflammation of the nasal passages (**rhinitis**) and erosions of the cartilage that separates the two nostrils of the nose (**perforated nasal**

septum). Crack, on the other hand, leaves other distinguishing marks. For example, **crack eye** refers to inflammation or ulcers the develop on the cornea (the outer lining of the eyeball that

THE CASE OF REGINA McKNIGHT

The case of one particular crack baby grabbed national headlines. Regina McKnight of South Carolina began to use drugs, including crack, after her mother was killed in a hit-and-run car accident. Regina was from a low-income family and had a poor educational background, with an IQ estimated to be 72. In 2001, Regina gave birth to a stillborn baby in South Carolina. Both she and her stillborn baby tested positive for cocaine, and Regina admitted to smoking crack numerous times during her pregnancy. Regina was reported to the local authorities, who charged her with "homicide by child neglect," alleging that it was Regina's crack use that killed her fetus. Regina was convicted of these charges in May 2001[41] after the jury had deliberated for only 15 minutes. She was sentenced to 12 years imprisonment, and despite numerous appeals to the state Supreme Court, she remains incarcerated to this day.

Regina's case is not without controversy, however. Many advocates for human rights, including those supporting pregnant women's rights such as the National Advocates for Pregnant Women (NAPW), argue that Regina should have been given access to social services and drug-treatment counseling instead of immediately being charged with a crime. They argue that Regina's case criminalizes motherhood, and that women who suffer stillborn births should not be viewed as murderers. They also question whether there is scientific proof that Regina's use of crack cocaine directly lead to her fetus' death. As of 2007, NAPW was assisting Regina in the appeal of her conviction. Supporters of her conviction, however, hold the view that pregnant mothers should be held responsible for the health of their fetuses, and that endangering the health of an unborn child by taking drugs should indeed be viewed as a crime in the eyes of the law.

covers the pupil) caused by chronic exposure of the eyes to crack vapors; these weakened areas can subsequently become infected by bacteria or viruses.[42] Chronic exposure to crack smoke can cause coarsening of the skin on the hands, and in people with longer fingernails (such as women), the crack vapors can cause a claw-like curvature of the nails.[43] Finally, habitual use of crack is often associated with **dental erosion**, in which tooth enamel and/or gums erode from the caustic nature of crack smoke.

As we mentioned in Chapter 1, some crack users crush crack rocks into small fragments and attempt to dissolve them over an open flame in order to draw the cocaine into a syringe and inject it intravenously. Crack-rock fragments are generally hard to dissolve in water, and crack users have found that adding a bit of lemon juice to the rock fragments helps them dissolve. This addition of lemon juice can cause irritation and damage to the veins where it is injected, and can also cause fungal infections of the eye (termed **Candida endophthalmitis**), which causes vision to deteriorate.[44]

In summary, repeated smoking of crack causes a host of psychological problems as well as numerous medical complications associated with the cardiovascular and respiratory systems. Cocaine use can also lead to excess weight loss and pathologies associated with the eyes, nose, mouth, kidneys, and skin. Crack use is associated with a high incidence of HIV infection and the development of AIDS, and crack use during pregnancy can cause damage to the fetus.

7

Prevention and Treatment of Crack Addiction

Mr. A (the elderly crack addict mentioned in Chapter 4) was initially referred to an outpatient psychiatric clinic for his depressed mood and excessive use of crack. This clinic provided counseling, during which Mr. A revealed that he held a significant grudge against his family members, who he felt did not treat him fairly during his divorce from his wife. Despite two years of counseling, Mr. A continued to be depressed and reported having thoughts of suicide. A crisis management team intervened on several occasions when they felt Mr. A might try to take his own life.

The psychiatrists at the clinic prescribed Mr. A antidepressants, plus prescription sleeping pills for insomnia. Despite this, Mr. A continued to smoke crack on occasion, and his family relationships further deteriorated when he revealed his continued drug use to them. Mr. A was then prescribed an individual program of cognitive behavioral therapy to encourage him to change his lifestyle and to teach coping skills for how to curb his cravings for cocaine. For several weeks during this treatment, his symptoms of depression seemed to improve, but he had difficulty remaining abstinent from cocaine, and six months later he unsuccessfully attempted suicide by taking an overdose of prescription pain relievers, sleeping pills, and alcohol. Mr. A was then remanded to an inpatient psychiatric facility for the elderly, where his mood improved and he improved his relationship with his family. Upon *discharge from the psychiatric facility, he stayed abstinent from crack for a few months, but then relapsed, and his depression and suicidal thoughts returned. Today he continues this pattern of being able to remain abstinent from crack and improved mood for several months, interspersed by relapses to using crack again and the return of suicidal thoughts.*

PREVENTION OF CRACK USE

Conventional wisdom would say the best way to kick a bad habit is to never start. This is especially true of using crack, since the drug is so highly addictive and difficult to quit once its use is initiated. Prevention of crack use is primarily aimed at children in elementary school, since the sixth or seventh grade is often the time when kids start to experiment with drugs. There are many drug education programs in the United States, including Drug Abuse Resistance Education (D.A.R.E.), the Partnership for a Drug-Free America, the Alcohol and Drug Awareness Program (ADAP), and TheAntiDrug.com. Drug education and awareness programs are designed to

- increase people's knowledge about the short and long-term effects of drugs

- improve self-esteem and self-image, since people with low levels of these traits are more prone to experiment with drugs

- to educate people about coping with peer pressure to use drugs

- to offer alternative after-school programs for at-risk youths to prevent involvement in drug use

- to increase parental involvement in children's activities.

- to keep schools drug free

Preventing crack use in adults is more challenging than in children because being out of school, they are harder to communicate with through outreach and education programs. In addition, adults tend to be more set in their habits and ways of life and less likely to change than children or adolescents. One way of preventing crack use in adults is the enforcement of strict laws regarding the possession and sale of crack, using fines and imprisonments as deterrents. Another method is by having schools require parents to take classes or otherwise become educated about the dangers of drug use if their children are caught becoming involved in drug use. Other attempts at educating adults about the harmful effects of crack include media ad campaigns and education programs through the workplace.

TREATMENT OF CRACK ADDICTION

The treatment of addiction to any drug is much more complex than obeying the slogan "Just Say No." Chronic drug use "rewires" the brain, changing its chemical and structural nature so that the addict is much more likely to continue to take drugs than he or she is to quit and remain drug free. There are many other factors as well that contribute to whether a crack addict will be successful in stopping the use of the drug, including social and family support, financial factors, and legal motivations to stay clean (e.g., avoiding jail). In addition, the recovery process is not an overnight occurrence. Treatment of drug addiction often takes months or years and is a very gradual process. Fortunately, there are many people and treatment facilities available to help the addict who wishes to get clean.

The first step in the process is **detoxification** (commonly called *detox*), where a drug user must abstain from taking cocaine under medical supervision while the body rids itself of the drug and all its metabolites. During detoxification, the crack user will experience severe symptoms of cocaine withdrawal: irritability and anger, depression, intense craving for the drug, fatigue, anxiety, lack of motivation, nausea and vomiting, tremors or shaking, muscle pain, and insomnia. Physicians will often prescribe mild sedatives such as Valium or other medications to help alleviate the symptoms of withdrawal. Following detoxification, the next step can be either behavioral therapy, pharmacological therapy, or a combination of both.

BEHAVIORAL THERAPIES

Drug addiction is not just a state of mind where a person is constantly cycling through drug-induced highs and the cravings for the drug once its effects wear off. Addiction is also a behavior, where one ritualistically engages in seeking out and ingesting the drug, paralleled by constantly seeking the financial resources to maintain the habit.

Some of the most effective treatments for addiction to crack cocaine are known as behavioral therapies, the goal of which is to change the overall behavior of the addict. One of these is called **contingency management** (also known as the community reinforcement approach). In this method, crack addicts who have been detoxified are rewarded for staying away from cocaine. At the end of a specific period of time (let's say three days), if a former addict does not use cocaine (this is usually verified by a blood or urine test), then he or she is rewarded with points. Accumulation of points allows for their exchange for prizes, such as movie tickets, tickets to a sporting event, vouchers for food or rent, or even opportunities for employment. The idea behind contingency management is to train the former addict to seek gratification from obtaining prizes or rewards that are not drugs. The prizes are always intended to be something that will improve the health and lifestyle of the recovering addict. If a relapse occurs, however, and the person tests positive for cocaine, he or she may lose points that have been earned.

Another type of behavioral therapy used in the treatment of crack addiction is called **cognitive behavioral therapy**, or CBT. This method attempts to change the way the addict feels and thinks about drugs. In frequent meetings with a counselor or behavior-modification therapist, the addict is educated about the harmful effects of drugs, and is taught coping skills for how to handle situations that may tempt them to take the drug or cause cravings for the drug. In addition, addicts talk with a counselor about the problems that led them to start using drugs (such as low self-esteem or depression) or what feelings they might be trying to escape by taking crack.

Another form of behavior treatment is what is known as a twelve-step program. Cocaine Anonymous, similar to Alcoholics Anonymous, is a program where cocaine addicts can get social support and help by group therapy with other cocaine addicts. The twelve-step program usually starts by having the addict admit that their addiction is a disease against which they are powerless, and must turn over their recovery process to God or a higher power for assistance. Spirituality often plays a large role in an addict's recovery process (as was the case for Marvin Wilson, who writes about the role of spirituality in defeating addiction to crack in his book, *I Romanced The Stone*). They also must make amends to people who were harmed or victimized by their drug use, and they must promise to try and assist others in their recovery. Twelve-step programs often use a "buddy" system, in which each addict is assigned a buddy or sponsor with whom he or she must check in regularly to ensure that drug taking has not resumed.

Contingency management, CBT, and twelve-step programs are often advantageous to crack users because they are done on an outpatient basis (where the addict comes and goes as he or she pleases) and are relatively inexpensive. In more severe cases of crack addiction, however, where the addict is uncooperative, skips appointments or meetings, or has a high rate of relapse, residential drug-treatment centers may be more effective. In such a facility the addict lives at the treatment facility (usually located in a suburban area away from the distractions of busy urban life) for months at a time, sometimes up to a year, where he or she is offered a broad range of counseling, behavioral, or medical treatments. Similar services are offered at certain psychiatric hospitals with specialized inpatient units for recovering addicts. Unfortunately, however, the costs of residential

Figure 7.1 Group therapy is an important part of the process of recovering from addiction. *(© Blair Seitz / Photo Researchers, Inc.)*

treatment programs or inpatient hospital stays are extremely expensive (up to $30,000 a month) and are not covered by most health insurance companies. This often makes them financially out of reach for many crack addicts who have spent every dollar they had on their drug habit.

PHARMACOLOGICAL THERAPIES

Addiction to crack is perhaps one of the most difficult to beat because there are no medicines currently available to help the addict in the recovery process. Various medications are approved in the United States for the treatment of alcoholism (including Antabuse, Vivitrex, and Campral), nicotine dependence and cigarette smoking (nicotine gums and lozenges, Zyban, and Chantix) or addiction to opiates such as heroin and morphine (Buprenex and methadone). Despite cocaine addiction having been recognized as a major medical and public health problem for several decades, there are currently no medications approved by the U.S. Food and Drug Administration (FDA) for the treatment of cocaine addiction in any form (crack, powder, etc.). Perhaps because of this, relapse rates for crack addicts are very high. Some doctors prescribe antidepressants such as Paxil, Zoloft, or Prozac to crack addicts to help them with any symptoms of depression they might have, but the effectiveness of these antidepressants in curbing actual crack use is not very high. The development of a pharmaceutical compound that would help curb a crack addict's craving for the drug would be a significant advance in the treatment of this powerful addiction.

There is, however, one medication that may provide some hope. A mild stimulant drug called modafinil (brand name Provigil) was approved in 1988 by the FDA for the treatment of various sleep disorders including narcolepsy. It is not known exactly how modafinil works in the brain. It appears to affect numerous neurotransmitter systems, and scientists are still investigating precisely how it affects the chemical communication between nerve cells in the brain.[45] Recent research has shown that this drug may actually help curb the use of cocaine.[46] In a very recent study conducted at Columbia University[47] on eight crack addicts (defined as people who used crack four or more days per week), researchers showed that modafinil reduced crack cocaine use as well as the high generated by crack itself. If larger research studies with more patients confirm that modafinil is effective at reducing crack use, craving, and rates of relapse, this may lead to one of the first medications being approved to help crack addicts get and stay clean.

In summary, the powerful addictive nature of crack cocaine makes it one of the most difficult addictions to treat. Prevention of its use is likely the best treatment of all, but in reality there will always be some people who cannot resist the lure of the drug's intense euphoria, and as a consequence there will likely always be crack addicts in need of treatment.

ANIMAL MODELS OF DRUG ADDICTION

In the latter half of the twentieth century, numerous animal models of drug addiction were developed and have proved invaluable in testing novel drug therapies for the treatment of addiction in humans. One of the most widely used methods to study drug addiction in animals is the intravenous self-administration model. In this model, a rat is implanted with a small piece of tubing called an intravenous catheter into one of its veins. After the rat recovers from the surgical procedure, it is placed in a special testing apparatus called an operant self-administration chamber. This chamber is equipped with two levers that are connected to a computer and a pump containing a syringe filled with a drug solution (e.g., cocaine). The rat is then trained to press one of the levers, which via the computer activates the syringe pump to deliver a small amount of cocaine solution through several feet of plastic tubing into the intravenous catheter in the rat. The second lever is inactive, and pressing it has no effect, which serves the purpose of forcing the rat to make a very specific response in order to receive the infusion of cocaine. The researcher conducting the experiment can then administer a test drug (like modafinil) to the rat to determine its effects on the rat's motivation to receive the cocaine infusions. Experiments using this type of procedure have shown to be very valuable in the development of pharmaceutical drugs to help in the treatment of drug addiction.

Psychological and behavioral therapies, combined with medications that curb craving for the drug, are the treatment options that are most likely to succeed. Continued research into how crack changes the chemistry of the brain, and how to "undo" these effects, will provide scientists with a significant challenge in their attempts to help people overcome addiction to crack cocaine.

Appendix 1

Drug Enforcement Administration Classification of Controlled Substances

In 1970, the U.S. government passed the Controlled Substances Act, which classified all drugs into one of five categories, or "schedules." In effect, this law classified drugs and other substances according to how medically useful, safe, and potentially addictive they are. These schedules are defined as follows:

Schedule I—(1) The drug has a high potential for abuse, (2) no currently accepted medical use in the United States, and (3) a lack of accepted safety. Peyote and mescaline are classified as a Schedule I substance, as are marijuana, heroin, Ecstasy, psilocybin, LSD, DMT, and Foxy.

Schedule II—(1) The drug has a high potential for abuse, (2) the drug has a currently accepted medical use in the United States or a currently accepted medical use with severe restrictions, and (3) abuse of the drug may lead to severe psychological or physical dependence. Cocaine, morphine, methamphetamine, and d-amphetamine are examples of Schedule II substances.

Schedule III—(1) The drug has less potential for abuse than the drugs in schedules I and II, (2) the drug has a currently accepted medical use in treatment in the United States, and (3) abuse of the drug may lead to moderate or low physical dependence or high psychological dependence. Anabolic "body building" steroids, ketamine, and many barbiturates are examples of Schedule III substances.

Schedule IV—(1) The drug has a low potential for abuse relative to the drugs in Schedule III, (2) the drug has a currently accepted medical use in treatment in the United States, and (3) abuse of the drug may lead to limited physical dependence or psychological dependence relative to the drugs or other substances in Schedule III. Antianxiety drugs such as Valium and Xanax, as well as prescription sleeping pills such as Ambien, Lunesta, Halcion, and Dalmane are examples of Schedule IV substances.

Schedule V—(1) The drug has a low potential for abuse relative to the drugs or other substances in Schedule IV, (2) the drug has a currently accepted medical use in treatment in the United States, and (3) abuse of the drug may lead to limited physical dependence or psychological dependence relative to the drugs or other substances in Schedule IV. Certain narcotic-containing prescription cough medicines such as Motofen, Lomotil, and Kapectolin PG are classified as Schedule V substances.

Notes

1. Wilson, Marvin D. *I Romanced the Stone.* St. Augustine, Fla.: Global Authors Publications, 2006: 61–67.
2. Ashley, Richard. *Cocaine: Its History and Effects.* New York: Warner Books, 1976.
3. Waninger, K.N., P.B. Gotsch, K.N. Waninger, D. Watts, and S.T. Thuahnai. "Use of lemon juice to increase crack cocaine solubility for intravenous use," *Journal of Emergency Medicine* (2007).
4. National Drug Threat Assessment. "Cocaine and Crack," National Drug Intelligence Center Report, (2003).
5. Chitwood, D.D., J.E. Rivers, and J.A. Inciardi. *The American Pipe Dream: Crack Cocaine and the Inner City.* Fort Worth, Tex.: Harcourt Brace College Publishers, 1996.
6. Samaha, A.N., and T.E. Robinson. "Why does the rapid delivery of drugs to the brain promote addiction?" *Trends in Pharmacological Sciences* 26 (2005): 82–87.
7. Foltin, R.W., and M.W. Fischman. "Self-administration of cocaine by humans: Choice between smoked and intravenous cocaine," *Journal of Pharmacology and Experimental Therapeutics* 261 (1992): 841–849.
8. Petersen, R.C. "History of cocaine," *National Institute on Drug Abuse Research Monograph* 13 (1977): 17–34.
9. Ruetsch Y.A., T. Boni, and A. Borgeat. "From cocaine to ropivacaine: The history of local anesthetic drugs," *Current Topics in Medicinal Chemistry* 1 (2001): 175–182.
10. No authors listed. "Classics revisited. Uber Coca. By Sigmund Freud," *Journal of Substance Abuse Treatment* 1 (1984): 206–217.
11. Drug Enforcement Administration. "Special report: The crack situation in the United States. Unpublished release from the Strategic Intelligence Section," Washington, D.C. (1986).
12. Office of National Drug Control Policy. "2001 Annual Assessment of Cocaine Movement," (March 2002).
13. Malcolm, Andrew H. "Crack, bane of inner city, is now gripping suburbs," *The New York Times,* October 1, 1989. Page A1.
14. Office of National Drug Control Policy. "National Drug Control Strategy FY 2006 Budget Summary," Washington, D.C. (2005).
15. 2006 National Drug Threat Assessment, National Drug Intelligence Center, United States Department of Justice, Document #2006-Q0317-001.
16. Cockburn, Alexander, and Jeffrey St. Clair. *Whiteout, the CIA and the Press.* New York: Verso, 1998.
17. Office of Applied Studies. "2002-2003 National Survey on Drug Use and Health (NSDUH), Substance Abuse and Mental Health Services Administration," Rockville, Md. (2003).
18. Drug Abuse Warning Network. "Annual Data 1983-1989, NIDA Statistical Series Numbers 3-9, National Institute on Drug Abuse," Rockville, Md. (1990).
19. Office of Applied Studies. "The Drug and Alcohol Services Information System (DASIS) Report: Cocaine route of administration trends: 1995-2005.

Notes

Substance Abuse and Mental Health Services Administration," Rockville, Md. (2007).

20. Kouimtsidis, C., and A. Padhi. "A case of late-onset dependence on cocaine and crack," *Addiction* 102 (2007): 666–667.

21. Office of Applied Studies. "2006 National Survey on Drug Use and Health. Substance Abuse and Mental Health Services Administration," Rockville, Md.

22. Metsch, L.R., H.V. McCoy, and N.L. Weatherby. "Women and Crack" in *The American Pipe Dream: Crack Cocaine and the Inner City,* D.D. Chitwood, J.E. Rivers, and J.A. Inciardi, eds.; Fort Worth, Tex.: Harcourt Brace College Publishers (1996): 71–88.

23. Davis, W.R., B.D. Johnson, H.J. Liberty, and D.D. Randolph. "Characteristics of hidden status among users of crack, powder cocaine, and heroin in central Harlem," *Journal of Drug Issues* 34 (2004): 219–244.

24. Mieczkowski, T. "Crack distribution in Detroit," *Contemporary Drug Problems* 17 (1990): 9–30.

25. Cross, J.C., B.D. Johnson, W.R. Davis, and H.J. Liberty. "Supporting the habit: Income generation activities of frequent crack users compared with frequent users of other hard drugs," *Drug and Alcohol Dependence* 64 (2001): 191–201.

26. Fischer, B., J. Rehm, J. Patra, K. Kalousek, E. Haydon, M. Tyndall, and N. El-Guebaly. "Crack across Canada: Comparing crack users and crack non-users in a Canadian multi-city cohort of illicit opioid users," *Addiction* 101 (2006): 1760–1770.

27. Bureau of Justice Statistics. "Substance Abuse and Treatment of State and Federal Prisoners, NCJ-172871, 1997. United States Department of Justice" (1999).

28. Bureau of Justice Statistics. "Substance Abuse and Treatment of State and Federal Prisoners, NCJ-209588, 2002. United States Department of Justice" (2005).

29. French, M.T., K.A. McGeary, D.D. Chitwood, C.B. McCoy, J.A. Inciardi, and D. McBride. "Chronic drug use and crime," *Substance Abuse* 21 (2000): 95–109.

30. Inciardi, J.A., and H.L. Surratt. "Drug use, street crime, and sex-trading among cocaine-dependent women: Implications for public health and criminal justice policy," *Journal of Psychoactive Drugs* 33 (2001): 379–389.

31. Inciardi, J.A. "Crack, crack house sex, and HIV risk," *Archives of Sexual Behavior* 24 (1995): 249–269.

32. McBride, D.C., and J.E. Rivers. "Crack and Crime," in *The American Pipe Dream: Crack Cocaine and the Inner City,* D.D. Chitwood, J.E. Rivers, and J. A. Inciardi, eds.; Fort Worth, Tex.: Harcourt Brace College Publishers (1996): 33–55.

33. Spunt, B.J., P.J. Goldstein, P.A. Bellucci, and T. Miller. "Race/ethnicity and gender differences in the drugs-violence relationship," *Journal of Psychoactive Drugs* 22 (1990): 293–303.

34. Goldstein, P.J. "The drugs/violence nexus: A tripartite conceptual framework," *Journal of Drug Issues* 14 (1985): 493–506.

35. Inciardi, J.A., D.C. McBride, H.V. McCoy, and D.D. Chitwood.

"Recent research on the crack-cocaine/crime connection," *Studies on Crime and Crime Prevention* 3 (1994): 63–82.

36. Drug Abuse Warning Network. "Historical Estimates from the Drug Abuse Warning Network. Advance Report No. 16. Department of Health and Human Services," Rockville, Md. (1996).

37. Drug Abuse Warning Network. "Emergency Department Trends From the Drug Abuse Warning Network, Final Estimates 1994-2001. DHHS Publication No. (SMA) 02-3635. Department of Health and Human Services," Rockville, Md. (2002).

38. Afonso, L., T. Mohammad, and D. Thatai. "Crack whips the heart: A review of the cardiovascular toxicity of cocaine," *American Journal of Cardiology* 100 (2007): 1040–1043.

39. Treadwell, S.D., and T.G. Robinson. "Cocaine use and stroke," *Postgraduate Medical Journal* 83 (2007): 389–394.

40. Daras, M., B.S. Koppel, and E. Atos-Radzion. "Cocaine-induced choreoathetoid movements ('crack dancing')," *Neurology* 44 (1994): 751–752.

41. State of South Carolina vs. Regina McKnight. South Carolina Court of General Sessions No. 00-GS-26–0432, 00-GS-26-3330; May 14–16, 2001.

42. Ghosheh, F.R., J.P. Ehlers, B.D. Ayres, K.M. Hammersmith, C.J. Rapuano, and E.J. Cohen. "Corneal ulcers associated with aerosolized crack cocaine use," *Cornea* 26 (2007): 966–969.

43. Payne-James, J.J., M.H. Munro, and C.M. Rowland Payne. "Pseudosclerodermatous triad of perniosis, pulp atrophy and 'parrot-beaked' clawing of the nails—A newly recognized syndrome of chronic crack cocaine use," *Journal of Forensic and Legal Medicine* 14 (2007): 65–71.

44. Albini, T.A., R.L. Sun, E.R. Holz, R.N. Khurana, and N.A. Rao. "Lemon juice and Candida endophthalmitis in crack-cocaine misuse," *British Journal of Opthamology* 91 (2007): 702–703.

45. Gerrard, P., and R. Malcolm. "Mechanisms of modafinil: A review of current research," *Neuropsychiatric Disease and Treatment* 3 (2007): 349–364.

46. Dackis, C.A., K.M. Kampman, K.G. Lynch, H.M. Pettinati, and C.P. O'Brien. "A double-blind, placebo-controlled trial of modafinil for cocaine dependence," *Neuropsychopharmacology* 30 (2005): 205–211.

47. Hart, C.L., M. Haney, S.K. Vosburg, E. Rubin, and R.W. Foltin. "Smoked cocaine self-administration is decreased by modafinil," *Neuropsychopharmacology* (2007, in press).

Glossary

acute—Symptoms that are short-term, intense, and have a rapid onset.

alveoli—Tiny air sacs in the lungs where substances can diffuse into the bloodstream.

aortic dissection—A tear in the wall of the aorta, the major artery carrying blood from the heart to the rest of the body.

anhedonia—Inability to feel pleasure.

axons—Long "fibers" of nerve cells that carry electrical signals from one nerve cell to another.

binges—Repeated takings of a drug every few hours over the course of a day or more.

Candida endophthalmitis—A fungal infection of the eyes.

cardiomyopathy—Heart disease in which the muscles of the organ become enlarged and stiff. This impairs the hearts ability to pump blood.

catheter—Small tube placed into a vein for delivery of a drug substance.

choreas—Involuntary movements, usually rhythmic in nature.

coca plant—Plant indigenous to South America from which cocaine is extracted.

cocaine hydrochloride—The most common form of cocaine; it appears as a white powder.

cognitive behavioral therapy—Form of behavioral therapy aimed at improving one's thought patterns (e.g., about the use of drugs) and teaching of coping skills (i.e., to help curb drug cravings or avoid situations that provoke the desire to use drugs).

contingency management—A type of behavioral therapy for drug addiction in which addicts accumulate points for staying off drugs; the points can be redeemed for prizes and privileges.

crack—Powerfully addictive form of cocaine; named for its rock-like appearance.

crack babies—Infants born to crack-addicted mothers.

crack dancing—Slang term for a neurological condition caused by use of crack cocaine that results in involuntary and uncontrollable movements of the arms, legs, fingers, toes, torso, or face.

crack eye—Abnormal ulcers or scars of the eye caused by fumes from crack cocaine.

crack house—Place where crack is bought, sold, smoked, or exchanged for sex.

crack lung—Scarring of the air sacs in the lungs due to chronic crack use.

crack pipes—Homemade devices with which one smokes crack cocaine.

delirium—Disorientation, lack of awareness of one's surroundings, inability to focus or shift one's attention, and memory loss.

delusions of grandeur—False beliefs associated with inflated sense of self-worth or invincibility.

dental erosion—Erosion of the tooth enamel or gums.

detoxification—Forced abstinence from drug use to allow the body to get rid of the drug and its metabolites.

dopamine—A chemical messenger within the brain thought to be involved in the sensation of pleasure and controlling voluntary movements.

drug czar—Director of the Office of National Drug Control Policy (ONDCP).

dyskinesias—Disorders of voluntary movement.

dysrhythmias—Irregular heartbeats.

economic compulsion—The need to resort to desperate and illegal measures (e.g., theft or robbery) in order to support one's drug habit.

frontal cortex—The forward part of the brain, involved in thinking, planning, and impulse control.

freebase—An extremely pure form of cocaine.

freebasing—The process of manufacturing or taking freebase cocaine.

hallucinations—False sensory perceptions, such as seeing or hearing things that are not really there.

hemorrhagic stroke—Rupture of a blood vessel in the brain, resulting in lack of blood supply to other parts of the brain.

hypertension—Increased blood pressure.

ischemic stroke—Blockage of blood supply to the brain.

metabolites— Products of the breakdown of a drug substance by the body.

myocardial infarction—When blood supply to the heart muscle itself is restricted or cut off; commonly called a heart attack.

Glossary

neurons—Nerve cells.

neurotransmitters—Chemical messengers used by nerve cells.

nucleus accumbens—One of the brain's "pleasure" centers.

paranoia—A delusional belief of anxiety or fear that one is being persecuted, plotted against, pursued, or followed, although there is no factual evidence to support this belief.

paste—Form of cocaine made when coca leaves are ground up into a pulp and dried.

perforated nasal septum—Erosion of the cartilage that divides the two nostrils of the nose.

platelets—Specialized cells in the blood that help form clots.

platelet aggregation—"Clumping" together of platelets in the blood.

primary market areas—Geographic areas where cocaine is primarily imported, distributed for sale, and used.

psychoactive—Having mind- and thought-altering properties.

psychosis—A mental state characterized by a loss of touch with reality, hallucinations, delusions, and disordered thought patterns.

pulmonary embolisms—Abnormal clotting of blood vessels in the lungs.

receptors—Specialized proteins localized on the surface of nerve cells that recognize specific neurotransmitters.

renal failure—Failure of the kidneys to function properly.

rhabodomyolysis—Abnormal breakdown of muscle tissue.

rhinitis—Irritation or inflammation of the nasal passages.

schedules—Classification of drug substances used by the Drug Enforcement Administration based on the medical usefulness of a particular substance and its potential to cause addiction.

seizures—Repeated involuntary contractions of the skeletal muscles of the body, often accompanied by loss of consciousness.

strokes—Damage to the brain or loss of brain function due to either the blocking of blood vessels that supply blood to the brain (ischemic stroke) or the rupture of blood vessels that supply blood to the brain (hemorrhagic stroke).

synapse—Junction between a nerve-fiber ending and a neighboring nerve cell.

synaptic terminal—Mushroom-shaped ending of a nerve fiber.

systemic model—The theory that crack is inherently associated with violent crime because of the violent nature of trafficking and sale of crack itself.

tachycardia—Faster-than-normal heart beat.

tactile hallucinations—False sensory perceptions pertaining to the skin, such as the sensation that tiny insects are crawling underneath one's skin.

tolerance—The phenomenon of the same dose of a drug having less of an effect after it is taken repeatedly; is thought to result from the body's adaptation to the continued presence of the drug.

transporters—Specialized proteins located on a synaptic terminal that reabsorb neurotransmitters after they are released.

ventral tegmental area—One of the brain's "pleasure" centers.

Bibliography

General
Carroll, M. *Cocaine and Crack*. (The Drug Library) Berkeley Heights, N.J.: Enslow Publishers, 1994.

Landau, Elaine. *Cocaine* (Watts Library) New York: Franklin Watts, 2003.

Chitwood, D.D., J.E. Rivers, and J.A. Inciardi. *The American Pipe Dream: Crack Cocaine and the Inner City*. Fort Worth, Tex.: Harcourt Brace College Publishers, 1996.

Reinarman, Craig, and Harry G. Levine, eds. *Crack in America: Demon Drugs and Social Justice*. Berkeley: University of California Press, 1997.

Chapter 6
Schneir, A., and A.S. Manoguerra. "Medical consequences of the use of cocaine and other stimulants." in *Handbook of the Medical Consequences of Alcohol and Drug Abuse*, J. Brick, ed; New York: Haworth Press, 2004, 257-279.

Chapter 7
Wallace, B.C. *Crack Cocaine: A Practical Treatment Approach for the Chemically Dependent*. New York: Brunner/Mazel, 1991.

Further Resources

Books
Bayer, Linda N. *Crack and Cocaine*. Philadelphia: Chelsea House Publishers, 2000.

Holmes, A., and Claire Reinburg. *Psychological Efffects of Cocaine and Crack Addiction*. Philadelphia: Chelsea House Publishers, 1998.

Inciardi, James A., Dorothy Lockwood, and Anne E. Pottiger. *Women and Crack-Cocaine*. New York: MacMillan Press, 1993.

Palenque, Stephanie M. *Crack + Cocaine = Busted!* Berkeley Heights, N.J.: Enslow Publishers, 2005.

Peck, Rodney G. *Crack*. New York: Rosen Publishing Group, 1997.

Robbins, Paul R. *Crack and Cocaine: Drug Dangers*. Berkeley Heights, N.J.: Enslow Publishers, 1999.

Roleff, Tamara L. *Cocaine and Crack*. San Diego: ReferencePoint Press, 2007.

Wagner, Heather L. *Cocaine*. Philadelphia: Chelsea House Publishers, 2003.

Web Sites
Cocaine Anonymous
http://www.ca.org

DEA Web Site on Drug Information
http://www.usdoj.gov/dea/concern/concern.htm

Drug Abuse Resistance Education
http://www.dare.com

NIDA for Teens Web Site
http://teens.drugabuse.gov

SAMHSA's National Clearinghouse for Alcohol and Drug Information
http://ncadi.samhsa.gov

National Institute on Drug Abuse (NIDA)
http://www.drugabuse.gov

National Youth Anti-Drug Media Campaign
http://www.theantidrug.com
http://www.freevibe.com

Office of National Drug Control Policy
http://www.whitehousedrugpolicy.gov

Partnership for a Drug-Free America
http://www.drugfree.org

Index

Index

Index

About the Author

M. Foster Olive received his bachelor's degree in psychology from the University of California, San Diego, and went on to receive his Ph.D. in neuroscience from UCLA. He is currently an assistant professor in the Center for Drug and Alcohol Programs and Department of Psychiatry and Behavioral Sciences at the Medical University of South Carolina. His research focuses on the neurobiology of addiction, and he has published in numerous academic journals including *Psychopharmacology* and *The Journal of Neuroscience*. He has also authored several books in the Drugs: The Straight Facts Series, including *Peyote and Mescaline, Sleep Aids, Prescription Pain Relievers,* and *Designer Drugs.*

About the Consulting Editor

David J. Triggle is a university professor and a distinguished professor in the School of Pharmacy and Pharmaceutical Sciences at the State University of New York at Buffalo. He studied in the United Kingdom and earned his B.Sc. in chemistry from the University of Southampton and a Ph.D. in chemistry at the University of Hull. Following post-doctoral work at the University of Ottawa in Canada and the University of London in the United Kingdom, he assumed a position at the School of Pharmacy at Buffalo. He served as chairman of the Department of Biochemical Pharmacology from 1971 to 1985, and as dean of the School of Pharmacy from 1985 to 1995. From 1995 to 2001, he served as the dean of the graduate school and as the university provost from 2000 to 2001. He is the author of several books dealing with the chemical pharmacology of the autonomic nervous system and drug-receptor interactions, some 400 scientific publications, and has delivered more than 1,000 lectures worldwide on his research.